THE PAST NEVER FORGETS

K.M. SCOTT

Connor Jennings has always aimed higher.

He wasn't meant to rot in that dying western Pennsylvania town or settle for a middling management job and a mortgage he can barely afford. He's got a wife, two daughters, and a future he's determined to secure, no matter the cost.

The past? That was another life. The reckless kid he used to be, the mistakes he buried right after high school? None of that matters now. He's not that person. Not anymore.

But when someone from that buried life suddenly reappears, Connor's carefully built world begins to crack. Because what he left behind didn't stay buried.

And this time, it's coming back for him.

2023, 2025 Eight Feathers Press

ISBN: 978-1-947705-10-4

Published in the United States

CHAPTER ONE

amie

My two daughters barely let me put the brakes on before they fling open the doors and jump out of the backseat of my Camry with their gym bags in tow. Thankfully, I'm already in a parking space, but I don't even get to shift the car into park before they're gone.

"Watch for cars!" I yell, but neither one is paying attention to me.

It's like this every day when I drive them to gymnastics practice. I appreciate their excitement, especially since their father routinely questions if we should bother continuing this afterschool activity. I just wish the two of them didn't have to run off like wild animals each time.

I sit for a few minutes, deciding whether or not I

should go relax at a coffee shop around the corner or sit and watch the practice. Most of the mothers attend every practice, as I have for the past two years, but now that the girls' spots on the team are secure, I think I can spare myself one gymnastics practice.

A tap on my driver's side window tears me from my deliberations, and I jerk my head to the left to see Maris Durante smiling at me. A somewhat attractive woman with nice teeth and big brown eyes, she has the misfortune of being married to a man who is nothing less than a complete jackass. A lawyer, he never fails to offend whenever he attends any of the team's get-togethers. I don't know how she puts up with him, to be honest.

I lower the window and smile at her. She really does have the loveliest almost black hair that falls halfway down her back. It's a little long for my taste, but she's the one who has to deal with it.

"Hey, Jamie! You going in?" she asks in her perky way.

"I'm thinking I want to go relax and have a coffee at that little shop down the road. Want to join me?" I ask, knowing the answer before I even say the words.

Horror fills her face for a few fleeting moments before she shakes her head and forces a smile. "Oh, no. You know how it is. Tiffanie always feels better when I'm there watching."

That's a lie, and Maris knows it. I doubt her kid even notices when she's there. None of them do. It's Maris who feels better when she's there because she knows that's the only way she can influence the coach.

She doesn't dare not sit through every minute of

practice today. Her daughter Tiffanie has been struggling for the past two months and hasn't been able to land a single vault in weeks, even though that's supposedly her best event. If she wants to stay on the team, her mother is going to have to be front and center schmoozing with the coach before the roster for the big meet at the end of the month is set.

That's how the world of children's sports works. I don't like it any more than anyone else. I certainly have better things to do than sit around with other parents and watch little girls jump around for hours, especially since most of their mothers peaked in high school, but if you want your kid to be noticed, then you need to make an appearance so the coach can see how committed you, and by extension, your children are about being on the team.

Not that my Cassandra and Danielle need that anymore. Thank God, they're gifted at the sport and have already secured their spots.

"Oh, okay," I say, forcing myself to look disappointed that she can't join me. "See you later!"

She hurries off to get a good seat on the bottom row of bleachers right in front of the coach. I doubt it's going to do much good, but I have to give it to her. She does what's necessary to make sure her daughter has every chance to be on the team.

It's a beautifully sunny May day, already warm enough to be in the mid-eighties. As I drive over the streets that lead to the coffee shop, I pay attention to the tree line on Park Street. I've always loved streets that have a wonderful canopy above. My husband thinks that's simply a reason for people to want more for their houses, so we never even bothered looking at any with that feature when we were searching for a house to buy.

By the time I pull into the coffee shop's parking lot, I can feel myself grow irritable. It's a stupid thing, really. What does it matter if Connor decided all on his own that we couldn't live on a tree-lined street? Our home is beautiful. Newer than any house with that perk, it's got virtually everything I wanted in a new home and absolutely everything my husband demanded.

I love my house. I'm just being silly.

Just like Connor always says I am.

Walking into the coffee shop, I look up at the sign and see the first three letters of the word coffee are out on the sign. Well, it's still right, technically. We all pay a fee for our drinks.

I usually go through the drive-thru after the girls' practice, so I'm surprised to see the inside of the business is quite homey. A warm brown shade on the walls sets the tone and blends well with the dark brown tiles covering the floor. As I wait in line, I study the colorful framed posters of coffees from around the world hung on the walls.

Thankfully, once I finally get my coffee and blueberry scone, I quickly find a seat near the front window of the shop. Taking a deep breath, I relax after the frantic drive to gymnastics. Every day when I pick the girls up from school, they're wired like someone's been giving them caffeine and sugar all day. They talk nonstop to one another the whole ride across town to practice, never letting me get a word in edgewise. All I'd ask, if I could, would be how their school day was for them, but I never even get that chance.

I guess it's a good thing the girls have lots to talk about after a school day. They're both very popular in their classes, Cassandra having many friends in sixth grade and Danielle always in demand for sleepovers with fellow fifth graders. In fact, now that I think about it, I shouldn't worry at all. If they were outcasts and had no friends, those would be things to be concerned about, not being the most popular girls in their respective years.

With all of that running through my mind, I break off a piece of scone and pop it into my mouth. It's unbearably dry, so I quickly gulp down some of my coffee to get the bite of pastry to make its way down to my stomach. I know these things are supposed to be dry, but it's like this blueberry scone has dust coming off it.

"Those things are like the Sahara desert. They should give customers a warning before selling them."

I look up to see a woman holding a cup of coffee and a cookie and smiling down at me. Instantly, my attention is drawn to the scars that transect her face. One runs from the corner of her right eye to the outside of her nose, and another cuts the left side of her face in half. Makeup covers them, and it's a very good job, but the scars are raised, so it's impossible for her to completely conceal them.

Sure I'm staring at them, I force myself to look up at her eyes. Blue, they show a sadness her smile is trying to obscure. Her light brown hair hangs just below her shoulders, and other than being pin straight, it's unremarkable.

All of this races through my mind before I say to the woman, "They really are. I think next time I might get a glass of milk instead of coffee if I decide to get a scone."

The woman nods while her smile remains the entire time. I can't help but wonder what happened to her to leave those terrible scars, but the fact that she can smile about anything says they likely bother me far more than they bother her.

She motions toward the chair on the other side of my small table and asks, "May I join you?"

A quick glance around the shop tells me she might be lonely since there are at least four empty tables, but I don't mind the company. Chatting with someone is better than fixating on whatever thoughts pop into my head. Like my husband says, I become obsessed with too many silly things.

"Sure!"

She sits down, and just as I'm about to ask her name and tell her mine, she says, "I'm so sorry. I don't know where my manners are today. My name is Kelsey. Thanks for letting me sit with you."

I wave away the compliment since it was nothing to let her join me and say, "No problem. Nice to meet you, Kelsey. I'm Jamie. Jamie with the super dry scone."

That makes her laugh, and it's delightful, almost lyrical to my ears. "I learned my lesson a few weeks ago with those things. It's better if you have them heat it up and then put some butter on it. It helps moisten it, even if it's just a little."

"That's a great idea! I think I'm going to see if they'll pop mine into the microwave." Jumping up from my seat, I smile and say, "I'll be right back."

Thankfully, the young woman behind the counter obliges me since there's no one waiting in line, and a minute later, I return to the table to sit with my new friend and my hopefully slightly moister scone. Kelsey's busy enjoying a chocolate chip cookie with her coffee, and when I sit down, she once more smiles at me.

"I hope that fixes the problem for you."

After taking a bite of my now warm scone, I savor the butter flavor as it makes my mouth water, helping the scone to be as moist as I could ask it to be. "It's so much better!" I say with a mouthful of crumbs. "Sorry. My manners are usually much better, but I just got so excited that your trick worked."

Kelsey shakes her head like my concern about talking with my mouth full isn't something to even think about. "I'm just happy I could help. I like to pay things forward. One good turn deserves another my mother always liked to say. Thank God that woman told me about the butter that day she saw me sitting here struggling to wash down my scone, or we'd all be suffering."

Something in the way she talks reminds me of Connor, so I ask, "Are you from around here? I swear I hear some kind of accent, but I'm not sure. To be honest, you sound like my husband."

Her smile fades ever so slightly, making me think she's insulted by my question, so I quickly add, "I didn't mean to offend you. I'm sorry if I did."

I'm relieved when she shakes her head, but still her smile doesn't return. "It's okay. I think my parents' Pittsburgh accent rubbed off on me, even though I've never lived there. Is that what you're hearing?"

Excited I'm right, I nod my head. "Yes! My husband is from western Pennsylvania, and he has that accent too. It's slight nowadays, but when I first met him, it came through loud and clear."

"You should have heard my parents when they talked. They never lost that accent, even though they moved away from Pittsburgh before I was born."

That makes her chuckle, and her smile returns, brightening her face. In the very short time I've been around her, I already know I prefer when she's happy because those terrible scars look ten times worse when she's not smiling.

Our conversation falls silent for a minute or so as I eat the rest of my scone and she finishes her cookie. While I enjoy my treat, I study her. She's taller than I am. Then again, at five foot four, mostly everyone but children are taller than me. Her body is thin like mine, but something about her says she can eat whatever she wants while I'm going to have to watch my calories for the rest of the day because of my stop here.

What's most noticeable about her, though, is how stiffly she moves her head. I hadn't noticed it before, but as we sit together in silence, someone drops a glass on the other side of the coffee shop, and when she turns to look at what happened, it's like her entire upper body must turn at the same time. It reminds me of that time Cassandra hurt her neck in gymnastics and couldn't move her head for nearly a week.

"I guess he's cut off," she says with a chuckle, and when I don't laugh because I'm so transfixed by how she moves, Kelsey adds, "Well, maybe not since he's only drinking soda."

I realize she tried to make a joke, so I belatedly laugh, and that smooths things over once more.

"Do you come to this coffee shop often?" she asks. "I

am seriously addicted to caffeine, so I'm here all the time."

Taking a sip of coffee, I let the flavor sit on my tongue for a moment before swallowing and then answering, "I come here a lot too, but I usually do the drive thru since I have my daughters with me after practice."

That piques her interest, and she asks, "What kind of practice do your daughters have?"

"Gymnastics. Both Cassandra and Danielle are very talented gymnasts. They've already both made the team, so now I don't have to hang out and watch their practices. That means I can come here and actually see the inside of the building."

As I brag about my girls, Kelsey nods, as if she's actually interested in my family. "Oh, that's great. How old are they?"

"Twelve and eleven. We had kids very quickly one right after the other. We stopped after two."

I hope my unhappiness about that topic doesn't come through loud and clear. I've been trying very hard not to show people how much I wanted to have another child. Connor says it makes people uncomfortable.

But Kelsey doesn't seem to sense my long-simmering disappointment and gives me a big smile when she hears how old my daughters are. "Oh, that's a wonderful time in a girl's life. You know, before boys become the be all, end all. I remember being in fifth and sixth grade. Good times. My best friend and I would spend hours outside after school talking about everything under the sun."

There's a sadness in her voice as she talks about her

younger days, so I hurriedly change the subject. "Are you married? Any children?"

"I am. We couldn't have any children because of something that happened to me when I was a teenager. It's okay, though. My husband and I are very content with it being only the two of us."

I believe her when she says that. I don't know why, but I see true happiness in her eyes as she talks about her husband and their marriage. Knowing they likely can travel far more than Connor and I can because of the girls, I imagine she could be happier than me.

Not that traveling the world is better than having two wonderful daughters. I don't mean that at all. It's just that without children, I bet Kelsey and her husband get to enjoy a lot more freedom than Connor and I do.

"Do you travel much? I always think when the girls go off to college that we're going to go to Europe. My husband isn't entirely convinced he wants to yet, but it's Europe, for God's sake. I mean, Italy itself is reason enough."

Kelsey shrugs. "Not a lot. My husband would love to, but I'm not a good traveler."

As she finishes her answer, she covers the scar on the right side of her face with her hand. I have the feeling she doesn't like to travel because that would mean strangers reacting to her deformed face. I understand that. Fear of the unknown that can be a formidable opponent to living the life you want.

Before I can say another word, she stands up and gathers her coffee cup and napkin that came with her chocolate chip cookie. "I'm sorry, but I have to go now. I hope we can share a coffee another time, Jamie."

Sure my question about her traveling is the reason she's in such a hurry to leave, I nod excitedly. "Absolutely! I'm going to be stopping in here more now that I have a couple hours to kill when the girls are at gymnastics practice."

Kelsey smiles and nods her head. "Great! Then I look forward to seeing you again."

She leaves me feeling like I want to apologize for asking a question that bothered her so much. Since I can't, I'll be sure to look for her when I come here again.

It'll be nice to have another person to pass the time with.

CHAPTER TWO

onnor

THE GIRLS SQUEAL AND SHOUT OUTSIDE IN THE POOL as I try to read the news on my phone. Nothing but garbage. Doesn't anyone do anything good anymore? Why does it always have to be murders and people hurting one another? I'd kill for a story that involved someone fucking smiling.

Jamie putters around in the kitchen a few feet away from me making snacks for our daughters and their friends. This day is a celebration for both girls after both finishing in the top spots at practice this week. They've talked about nothing else but that and this party today since their mother suggested a celebration was in order. Four days of nonstop chatter about it, and then their mother jumps in with her ideas on how great the two of them did compared to the other girls.

It's enough to make a man wish he had a son or two to even things out.

That's not possible, unfortunately, but I still wish for it from time to time. Reality at the moment, however, is I have a beautiful wife who's given me two lovely daughters, and when I'm not trying to drown out their yelping and hollering, I'm the most grateful man in the world.

"Honey, do you think three bags of chips will be enough?" my wife asks, tearing me out of my thoughts.

I look up and shrug. I have no idea if three bags of chips will be enough for eight girls. Aren't they athletes? Should they even be eating chips? The thousand dollars I spend each month on gymnastics makes me wonder if my wife should have picked up some protein bars for them instead.

"Well, I thought it would be enough, but now as I stand here listening to them having such a good time out there, I wonder if they're going to be hungrier than I anticipated when I was standing in the junk food aisle at the store," Jamie says, punctuating her statement with a heavy sigh.

"I'm sure they'll be fine," I say as I sneak a glance down at my phone and some story about a local woman who found a shell estimated to be worth ten thousand dollars.

For a shell? What the hell kind of shell is it? Did someone famous used to own it, or is it from the time of the dinosaurs? Christ, why don't I ever find shit like that?

"I don't know," she says, continuing this conversation. "Maybe I should run to the store and get more. I do have a bag of pretzels and some of those pizza bagels the girls love. Well, Cassandra loves them. Danielle only picks at them every time I make them for sleepovers."

Already, I've heard enough about how much my two daughters eat. Neither one of them is more than a hundred pounds soaking wet. I doubt they need as much food as my wife thinks they do. As for the other kids, I don't care. Let them go back to their own homes to eat if they don't like what we're serving here.

I don't dare say that to my wife. She'll practically fall apart at the mere mention of not caring about what six pre-adolescents think. Then she'll give me the lecture on how important it is for the girls' success in gymnastics for them to be seen in a positive light, and the best way to do that is to have their teammates over as often as possible and show them a wonderful time.

It's keeping up with the Joneses on a level even the most ridiculous social climber could never imagine.

She acts as if they'll be ostracized if our house isn't nice enough and we don't entertain the little darlings to their hearts' content. Jamie nearly had a conniption one time when I mistakenly used the downstairs bathroom while three of their little friends were over one Saturday night. With tear-filled eyes, she explained I should have used our bathroom off our bedroom if I had to go. I wanted to ask if the little darlings are too delicate to deal with the faint scent of a man having used the toilet, but I did what I always do when my wife starts in on one of her things.

I nodded and smiled before kissing her cheek and walking away. There's no point in fighting with her on most of her crazy ideas. I'd only end up getting a long, drawn-out lecture about how I don't care about my daughters' well-being and happiness.

"Whatever you think is best," I mumble as I scroll through the sports section of the news.

Then I realize if she does make a trip back to the store, I'll be forced to watch eight pre-teen girls. Oh, no. Not happening. I did not sign up for that when I agreed our daughters should have some friends over.

Quickly, I jump up from my chair and stuff my phone into my pocket as I hurry into the kitchen. "Honey, why don't you let me run to the store for you? Just tell me everything you want me to get so the girls can be happy, and I'll get it all. Easy, right?"

She studies my face for the briefest moment before smiling at my suggestion. "Oh, thank you, Connor. I really appreciate you helping me with this. I'll write a list of everything I think we need. Just give me a minute."

Leaning in, I kiss her on the cheek before turning to walk upstairs. "My pleasure, honey. I need to put some shoes on, so I'll be back down in a minute."

I sometimes wonder if she knows I use these thoughtful errands as a chance to escape what she insists on doing around here. If she does, she hasn't said anything about it. I doubt she knows. My wife, while a beautiful woman, isn't exceptionally bright when it comes to seeing the truth of things in our life. It's the secret to how she's able to walk around with a smile all the time. Nobody's that happy, but she always appears to be completely content.

When we first got serious, I liked that about her. It made my life easier, so why shouldn't I appreciate having someone who only saw the positives? It was one of the main reasons I wanted to marry her. While other men had nagging girlfriends and wives, or worse, women who constantly wished for more than my friends could give them, I had a perfectly content woman happy as a clam to marry me.

It's become a trait I resent now, but not for the reason most people would think. It isn't the apparent happiness that's the problem. It's how she uses it as a way to do things I hate. It bugs me that despite the fact that she has no job, she spends like a sailor on leave to make our house look more impressive to others and to make the girls seem like they come from far more money than we have. Whenever I say anything about it, she simply smiles and answers, "Don't you want to be surrounded by nice things? A happy wife leads to a happy life, Connor."

And that right there is the thing I hate most. Her happiness being more important than mine because if she's not happy, then none of us will be. Who the hell came up with that nonsense? Why isn't it a happy husband leads to a happy life? Is it because it doesn't rhyme?

Ridiculous.

I mull all of this over as I sit on the edge of our king size bed and slip my sneakers on. Looking around the room, I see nothing I wanted here. It's all very Town and Country and nothing that I'd ever want my bedroom to be, but Jamie claims it's necessary, so it matches the rest of the house.

As if anyone who comes to visit us ever walks

upstairs to inspect our bedroom to make sure it's not clashing with the other twenty-six-hundred feet.

Closing my eyes, I stop myself from this spiral of discontent I get into sometimes. I have a very nice life. It's more than I could have ever imagined as a kid growing up in western Pennsylvania. I've traded miserable winters for the relative warmth of southern Maryland, left behind a life of lower middle class struggling for a well-paying job as a salesman that's given me the opportunity to have this beautiful, nearly three thousand square foot home with an in-ground pool in a gated community complete with tennis courts and nature trails only my neighbors and I can enjoy, and married a beautiful woman teenage me would have never been able to dream of getting.

Life is good, especially considering what it could have been because of that one mistake I made right before I turned eighteen.

I shake my head to stop my mind from returning to that night. I won't think of that today. I'm happy and don't need to remember anything from before I became this Connor Jennings. The person I was before isn't me now. That person wouldn't even recognize my life it's so changed from what it was then.

And that's the way it needs to stay. In the past. Never to be brought up again.

As I walk into the grocery store, I glance down at the list Jamie gave me. She should have been a doctor with handwriting like hers. Other than the additional bags of chips, I can barely understand a single thing on this paper in front of me. I should have asked her about it before I left, but I was in such a hurry I didn't have time. The last thing I wanted was to be cornered by one of my kids on my way out. Like their mother, my daughters think only of what I can buy them.

I squint as I try to make out some of the items my wife wants. Is that first line gummy bears? All those girls seem too old for that kind of candy, but what do I know? The next line might be vanilla ice cream. I remember her and the girls making ice cream sundaes a few months back and them dumping those colored gummy bears over the top, so that would make sense.

Looking up, I barely have time to step out of the way of a harried looking woman with her blond hair up in a bun rushing down the aisle. Jesus, slow down, lady. What's the hurry?

A man behind her passes by and gives me a tiny smile as if he's thinking the same thing. In a split second, I decide they're together. I don't know why I think that because she's got to be at least a decade younger than him. Or maybe he's just prematurely gray. I can understand that. I found my first gray hair a few weeks ago. Right near my left temple. I'm only thirty-six, but I'm already beginning to go gray.

When she turns around at the end of the aisle, she snaps, "Gregory, we're in a hurry. Our son and daughter are expecting us to be finished here and all set up for the end of their cello lessons. At the rate you're going, they'll already be first and second chair by the time we get out of here."

I watch his jaw tighten as he grits his teeth and hurries to catch up to her when she turns to walk to the next aisle. That's the kind of marriage I'd hate. See, there's a woman who nags. No doubt about that. I'd venture to guess she does even more than nag. She hectors him. I bet he never intended on his life being this miserable. It just happened. One day he was the man of the house with a wife and two children, and the next he was some jackass whose wife publicly humiliates him at the grocery store.

Yes, I really do have a good life. I need to remember that more often.

If only I could read my wife's chicken scratch she calls handwriting. Oh well. She and the girls will have to be happy with what I bring back.

I roll up to the register with a cart of things that might have been on the list and begin unloading items onto the conveyor belt behind an elderly man who's stacked his cans of dog food three high and six wide. I watch as he keeps a careful eye on them, moving once and then twice when he thinks they're about to tumble into a heap right before they get to the cashier. He's an odd-looking guy too with dark eyes that bug out a little too much and a strangely small nose for a man. Then again, it may only seem tiny because of those bizarre googly eyes. Reminds me of an older neighbor who used to live down the street from me when I was growing up, except Mr. Danson wasn't as tall as this man.

"I like things to be orderly," he says without a hint of guilt when he looks back at me.

With a smile, I pretend like he's not the oddest duck I've seen all day and keep piling up the items from my cart. The cashier tries to make small talk with him, asking about what kind of dog he has, but the man simply nods and points at the cans like he wants her to scan faster.

The grocery store is sure full of weirdos for a Saturday afternoon.

Ten minutes later, I'm all checked out and pushing my cart full of bags toward the store exit when I see the dog guy stop dead and point at some woman in the self-checkout area. He seems even more excited than he was about the way his dog's food was stacked a few minutes ago.

For a moment, I consider stopping to ask if he's okay, but the last thing I need is to be stuck here at the grocery store for God only knows how long while this guy has his attack or whatever it is. I've got two gallons of vanilla ice cream to get home and into the freezer.

I walk past him and glance over at a woman with dark hair and sunglasses. She looks like she's staring at him, but I realize it's not the old man she's interested in.

It's me.

My ego pleased I still have it, I smile at her, but then I notice something about her that makes my heart skip a beat. She looks so much like someone from my past.

Someone from back there, back where I left.

But that's impossible.

CHAPTER THREE

onnor

ALL THE WAY HOME, I TRY NOT TO THINK ABOUT THAT woman, but it's like her face is tattooed on my brain. Dark hair. Big sunglasses. Straight, white teeth like she wore braces for years when she was young.

No, that's impossible. My mind is playing tricks on me. She couldn't have been standing in the self-checkout area of my neighborhood grocery store. She's dead.

This is because I let my mind go back to that night all those years ago. I knew this would happen sometime. My brain would get the best of me, and then I'd be fixated on all that happened. Dammit! I've been so good for so long. Why is this happening now?

I pull into the driveway as I decide it's stress. Work has been a fucking bear lately. Between those two new guys coming out of the gate and making sales most of us haven't seen in two or three years and my boss Martin practically breathing down all our backs to do better this quarter, I've been a huge ball of stress from head to toe.

And Jamie hasn't been much help. Between her saying we need to find a new school for the girls since they've outgrown their current gymnastics teacher, which means I'll have to fork over more money for those damn sessions each week, and her claiming we need to hire a landscaper to make the yard look as good as all our neighbors' yards, I've had to listen to a near constant stream of we need talk for the past month or so.

Yes, it's definitely stress. My mind is playing tricks on me. I couldn't have seen who I thought I saw. Not possible. Dead people don't hang out at the grocery store.

I chuckle at that idea and silently joke to myself that they don't use self-checkout either. A dead person would definitely use a regular checkout. I mean, if they're dead, the last thing they want to do is scan their own damn items. Hell, most living people don't want to do that.

Pinching the bridge of my nose, I close my eyes and take a deep breath. The stress is getting to me. I need to get my head together. In two minutes, I have to deal with my wife and eight screaming girls. It was just my mind playing games with me. That's it.

After grabbing the four grocery bags, I head into the house where my daughters and all their friends have set up camp in the living room. I level my gaze on Jamie as if to ask, "Why the hell aren't they outside?" but she doesn't understand my look and simply hurries over to grab the bags out of my hands.

"Girls, look what Mr. Jennings got! Ice cream,

gummy bears, the works! Let's get this party started!" she squeals, and I swear she sounds just like one of the preteens surrounding me.

That gets eight girls even more excited and jumping up and down. As I look on in horror while they rush into the kitchen, I have to wonder if they really need more sugar.

What I need is to get the hell away from this before the headache that started forming on the drive home explodes into a full-on throbbing migraine. With a quick wave, I hurry upstairs to change my shoes. By the time I sit down on the edge of the bed, I feel trapped in my own home. I could go downstairs to my home office, but all that goddamned yelling is going to make concentrating on anything impossible. Even all the way up here I can hear them.

Three thousand square feet of house that I pay far too much of my salary for each month and I'm stuck hiding out in my bedroom in order to get some peace and quiet. Someone remind me again why having kids is such a joy.

Jamie interrupts my attempt at silence, bursting into the bedroom like some frantic chicken. "Oh, Connor! The party is such a hit! This is going to help the girls so much. You watch!" she squeals as she searches the room for something.

"Great. What are you looking for?"

She spins around, and I see her hands full of the towels she bought a few months ago that cost a fortune. "I need more towels for the girls."

"What's wrong with the beach towels they've been

using for the past couple hours? Why do they need our good towels?"

Stopping in front of me, she shakes her head as her eyes fill with tears. What the hell is she so emotional about? I merely asked about towels.

"Don't you want your girls to be popular? Their friends are going to tell their parents about what they saw at our house, and I don't want them saying that they had to use those beach towels the whole time they were here. Don't worry. I'll wash them after they're done."

I watch her scurry away as I shake my head in disbelief. I don't understand her. Are these darlings too good for beach towels?

Whatever. I can't be bothered to dissect my wife's thinking. Let her deal with all of them and all of the nonsense involved with impressing their parents.

Maybe I can get out on the links for a few holes of golf so I can escape all of this. My temporary moment of hope is dashed when I remember hearing that there wasn't a tee time available until two weekends from now. Something about the club inviting in more members creating a backlog on reservations.

So that shoots down that idea. I need to think of something to get me as far away from a house full of girls as possible.

My mind remains blank for a few minutes as the yelping from downstairs makes thinking next to impossible. Jesus, don't these girls ever stop? You'd swear someone was strangling them in my living room.

Then an idea comes to me. Bryan from the office mentioned something about doing something this weekend. What the hell was it? Hiking? Cycling?

Dammit, why didn't I pay attention when he was going on and on about it the other day during morning break?

I know the reason. He's always talking about doing something with his time off, and I swear to God it takes every ounce of strength I have not to be filled with jealousy. I don't know if he's married, but if he is, his wife isn't like mine. That's for sure. I can't remember a weekend in the past six months that she didn't have something planned that interrupted any chance I had to relax.

My envy of his life aside, if he's got something good going on, maybe I can join him and get away from here for a while. Kill two birds with one stone, so to speak.

With new hope that I won't be trapped here all day with eight screaming preteen girls and a squealing woman, I fish my phone out of my shorts pocket and search for his number. There's no Bryan in my contacts, though. Christ, what did I list him under? I scroll up and down through the names until one jumps out at me finally.

Guy From Work. Not exactly the most complimentary description I've ever given someone. A little bland, in fact, but certainly not the worst I've called people.

A few seconds later, his phone begins to ring, and I hope beyond hope he'll give me some excuse to get away. Even biking would be a welcome relief from what I'm dealing with here.

"Hey, Connor! Fancy you calling me right now. Did you decide to take me up on my offer to go hiking?" Bryan asks with almost as much enthusiasm as my wife.

"Yeah. I thought some fresh air might be good for me."

"Great! Meet me at the community center in ten minutes. Be sure to wear the right kind of shoes. It's not incredibly mountainous around here, but it still can leave you with a twisted ankle if you aren't careful."

"Got it. Hiking boots it is."

"And no shorts. I know you like to wear them, but with all the things out on the trails, you need long pants."

"Long pants. Check. Anything else?"

Bryan hums into the phone for a few moments before answering, "Nothing I can think of. Just be sure to be ready for a workout. After, we can grab a few drinks since the bar at the clubhouse will be next to empty by the time we get back. Sound good?"

What it sounds like is a chance to escape the insanity of my estrogen-filled home for a few hours. Hiking isn't exactly the way I prefer to spend my weekend afternoons, but I'll take it today.

"Sounds great!" I say in my best fake excitement voice.

"Cool! See you in ten at the community center."

Happy to have something to save me from what my house has become, I toss my phone on the bed and hurry to find a pair of comfortable long pants I can wear on this hike. All my pants are for work, but I think I might have one pair that will do. Stepping into the walk-in closet my wife and I share, I'm surrounded by her clothes. I look to the left to see a tiny section of mine shoved into a corner. This must be another example of that happy wife, happy life stuff.

It takes me a few minutes to find my tan pants stuffed

into a cubby in the back of my section. When I take them out and see they're wrinkled, I'm instantly infuriated. The neighbors' kids can't use anything less than towels made of fine Egyptian cotton, but my clothes can be jammed into the closet in practically a ball?

I open my mouth to yell for my wife to come up here, but what's the point? She'll only explain how important it is for her to be downstairs doing her best helicopter mom routine while she tearfully stares at me like I'm some madman who doesn't care about his children.

Forget that.

When I slip my right leg into the pants, I notice they aren't too wrinkled once I'm in them. Maybe this won't be bad, after all. I'm still pissed, but I'll discuss that with Jamie later.

I find my brown hiking boots crammed into the back of the closet like my pants were. Lifting them out of their cubby, I can't help but glance at the way her dozens of shoes are carefully placed along the shelf dedicated to only them.

Must be nice to take care of something.

Five minutes later, I'm dressed and ready for a hike. Maybe it will clear my head a little and put me into a better mood. Between my wife and those girls downstairs and that weird experience at the grocery store, I need something to help this day improve.

I breeze through the living room on my way toward the front door and call out to my wife in the kitchen, "Going out! Be back later!"

Unfortunately, she can't just yell back, "Have a good time!" No. She has to rush toward me as I head out, saying, "Wait! Connor, I need to talk to you."

Ten to one she doesn't actually need to talk to me. She just wants to say something about some stupid idea she's concocted about doing something to make the girls more popular.

I turn to face her, hoping she sees the expression of disgust on my face. I don't ask for much. I just don't want to be involved in any of the nonsense she has going with these kids. Why can't she understand that?

When I don't ask her what she needs, she narrows her eyes and tugs her eyebrows in toward her nose to give me that face that says she's upset I'm not interested in what she has to say. Normally, I'd give her what she wants, but one glance down at my still somewhat wrinkled tan pants makes me want to do nothing of the sort.

"Where are you going? I'm here with a houseful of girls. I need you here."

"First of all, I never wanted any of these girls here, and before you ask me if I care about our daughters and how not having this party could hurt them socially, know this. I don't care right now. What I care about is the fact that in a closet the two of us are supposed to share, my clothes are stuffed into a corner so they're wrinkled as shit. See these pants, Jamie? I have to wear them like this because you treated them like garbage."

She looks down at my legs and then up at me in pure horror. "You can't leave the house in them! They're wrinkled. What will people think?"

Already sick of this conversation and everything about this day, I snap, "They'll think my wife doesn't take care of my things as well as she does her own, and you know what? They'd be right. Now move so I can leave. I don't know when I'll be back. Have fun with the girls."

Jamie stands staring at me, her mouth hanging open in shock as I do just as I said I would, flinging the front door open and marching out into the sunlight in my wrinkled pants. I don't care what people think. If anyone dares to ask, I'll tell them the truth and I won't feel one ounce of shame about it.

As I start the car to drive to the community center a few blocks away, I glance over at the front door and see my wife still standing there in utter shock that I'm leaving. Did she expect me to stay at home all day with eight girls doing their best pterodactyl impressions? Maybe if she had asked me if I wanted to help I might have, but since I wasn't even consulted about today's social event, I see no reason why I should stick around and be miserable.

She can have the social climbing all to herself. She loves that stuff anyway, so why not?

CHAPTER FOUR

amie

ONE BY ONE, PARENTS PICK UP THE GIRLS WHO'VE been our guests for the past few hours. Tiffanie asked to have Cassandra and Danielle sleep over tonight, but I want to make sure Maris is okay with that before just herding my daughters out to her car when she arrives.

As she opens her car door, she waves up at me standing on the front porch. "How did the party go? I'm thinking they all drove you crazy since you're out here," she says with a laugh.

I quickly move to show her that's not the reason I'm waiting for her at all. "Oh, no. We love having the girls' friends over. I wanted to grab you before Tiffanie saw you because she asked Cassandra and Danielle if they wanted to sleep over your house tonight. I figured we should settle things before the girls come out and start begging."

Maris nods as I hurry to explain I didn't dislike having all the girls from gymnastics over today. "Oh, that works well for me, actually," she says with a big smile. "Michael took Brennan on a Cub Scout camping trip this weekend, so it's just Tiffanie and me at the house. It'll be nice to have more people around until they get back."

"That's great! I know the girls will all be thrilled. Let me go tell them to get their things ready. Come in and sit down. We can chat while the girls are packing their stuff for tonight."

We walk inside and inform our daughters that the sleepover can happen, and the three of them run to Danielle's room to pack their bags. As I clean up, I pour Maris a glass of diet soda.

Before I hand her it, I ask, "Do you want a glass of wine instead?"

She waves off my question and takes the soda. "No, not since I'm driving. Even a single glass can mess me up, and I'd be beside myself if any of the girls got hurt."

I smile and nod like I agree with her, but we live in the same development, and her house is only three streets over. I doubt she could gather up enough speed that would endanger the girls in the time that it takes to go from here to there.

As much as I like Maris, I wonder if I should tell her that this teetotaling attitude of hers won't help her with the other mothers who are very much people who drink wine no matter what time of day it is. Thankfully, I enjoy my wine, so they've never had any issues with me, but I just know they'll eat her alive if they hear her say no when they offer.

Even worse, they'll make sure Tiffanie never gets anywhere on the team or in school if they don't like Maris. If she wants to help her daughter, she better start learning the rules of this game.

All of this marches through my head, but I decide not to say anything to her. Better for me to look after my own girls' futures. Her daughter's potential success or failure isn't my responsibility.

It's hers.

"Did Connor stay for the party?" she asks, tearing me out of my thoughts about poor Tiffanie and her future.

I shake my head but make sure to paste a smile on my face. Maris may not be like the other mothers, but I don't want her thinking my husband doesn't care about his girls either, no matter how much she might understand.

"No, he had to go out to handle something for work," I lie before turning my back to her so even if my expression wants to tell the world Connor isn't all I wish he could be, she won't see that.

"I tell Michael all the time he's missing out when he's not around for these parties the girls have. He says Brennan is the child he handles, so Tiffanie is the one I can handle."

As I gather up bowls of chips and pretzels, I glance over at her and shrug. Maris's husband isn't the worst man in the world. Yes, he has a tendency to be an obnoxious know-it-all, but he goes to every Cub Scout meeting or campout and every baseball game for their son, and I've never seen him once look miserable when he comes to the gymnastic meets. I'd be happy if Connor did half of that for either of our girls. Michael is just a horse's ass, but in the grand scheme of things, I guess that's not the worst thing a man can be.

Eager to move away from the subject of our husbands, I set the dirty bowls down on the counter and look into the dining room when I ask her, "What are you and Michael planning to do with the kids for the summer? We're thinking at least one camp, but we haven't decided yet."

Maris sighs and takes a sip of diet soda before answering, "We aren't sure either. Brennan wants to go to baseball camp, but that would leave Tiffanie out, and Tiffanie wants to go to dance camp, but that would leave Brennan out. I guess we could send them to two different camps, though."

I silently wonder if it's the cost of both camps that is concerning her. Michael has a good job in the federal government that brings in more than enough money, or at least I think it does. I honestly can't imagine things are so tight that they can't afford two camps this summer. She's lucky. I never know about Connor's job, which seems to swing between feast and famine and constantly has me on pins and needles regarding the amount of money we'll have month to month.

"What are you thinking of doing with the girls for camp?" she asks, interrupting my silent complaining about my husband.

"Oh, I'm thinking dance camp. Danielle especially wants to go. Cassandra has always been more athletic, so she'd like something more intense, but I think she'll enjoy dance camp all the same."

That makes Maris suddenly perk up. With a big smile, she says, "Then it's settled! I'll tell Michael that Tiffanie has to go to dance camp. She'll be thrilled when she finds out your girls will be attending too."

Before I can say another word, the three girls come charging into the dining room with their sparkly pink and purple backpacks ready to leave for the sleepover. They all chatter at the same time, so nobody can understand a word they're saying.

Finally, I raise my voice and announce, "Girls, girls, if you're ready and Tiffanie's mother says she's ready to go, then you can start your big night out."

Immediately, all three girls train their attention on Maris, so she quickly stands up and hands me her glass of soda. "I'm ready. You ladies are going to have the best time. We're having pizza delivered, and we've got all the streaming packages, so you'll have hundreds of movies to choose from."

That makes the three of them scream and jump up and down. God bless Maris because I don't think I could handle a night filled with that this weekend after today.

"Okay, girls, come over here and give me a hug before you get started on this night of pizza and movies!" I say, opening my arms in preparation for my daughters to say goodbye.

Danielle hurries over and not only gives me a hug but a kiss too. "Will you miss us tonight, Mom? Are you and Dad going out to eat since we'll be at Tiffanie's house?"

I push her dark hair off her face and kiss her forehead. "We'll see. You just have a good time, and I'll be over to get you before lunch tomorrow."

My older daughter seems disinterested in hugging or

kissing me, but she comes over and gives me one of her half-hearted hugs before turning away as she says, "It's only one night, Mom. We aren't going away for weeks."

Sometimes I wonder if teen angst has arrived early with Cassandra. Whatever it is, she can be a bit surly lately. She always has taken after her father more than me.

"Well, I'll miss you anyway."

Maris herds them out of the dining room, and with a final wave, takes them all out of the house, leaving me in perfect silence. I let out a heavy sigh, happy to finally have some peace and quiet.

Looking around, I estimate I have about an hour's worth of cleaning up to do after eight, very excitable girls spent hours eating, drinking, and swimming. I glance up at the clock in the dining room and see it's nearly four o'clock. Connor's been gone for over two hours. Something tells me he isn't planning on coming back anytime soon since he's likely thinking our daughters and all their friends are still here.

Resentment starts to fill me at the very thought that he's avoiding being here because that would mean he had to be a part of the girls' big day. Is it really that much hassle to support me in my efforts to make sure the girls are popular? For years, I've sat through every single practice for every activity they've ever done. Gymnastics, cheerleading, art classes, you name it, they've done it and I've been right there, front and center so the coaches and organizers knew the girls had my support. Yet, he's never had to be at anything. He never even attended the year-end parties or parents' nights.

But, oh God help all of us if the girls weren't popular

because Connor would say that reflects badly on him at work. Maybe he should try helping me sometimes then.

"The hell with him," I mumble under my breath as I toss the plastic bowls in the sink. "If he comes home and the place is a mess, maybe he can do something to clean it up."

With a head full of steam, I march upstairs to grab my purse and then with irritation filling me, I hurry outside to my car. My husband thinks he's the only one who gets to have an afternoon away. Well, he's wrong, and he's about to find out how much he's mistaken.

Ten minutes later, I park the car in a spot near the front door to the coffee shop. It'll be nice to enjoy a leisurely cup of coffee and a scone, heated with butter, of course, just like Kelsey told me about. Maybe she's here today. It might be nice to have her join me again.

I just hope I don't run into any of the mothers from gymnastics. I don't think I could pull off my happy and contented wife routine right now.

When I enter the shop, I don't see my new friend, unfortunately. That's okay, though. A nice relaxing cup of coffee by myself is good too.

"Hi, Mrs. Jennings," the young blond lady behind the counter says with a big grin. "What can I get for you today?"

I don't know why, but hearing her refer to me that way bothers me. She's never heard me tell her my first name, so naturally she can't call me by that, yet the name she called me makes me want to let her know who I am.

"Please, call me Jamie. Mrs. Jennings sounds so formal."

For a moment or two, she looks surprised, like very

few people bother to give them their name. Then she smiles again and says, "Okay, Jamie. How are you today? What can I get you?"

That little business straightened out, I look up at the board above her head that lists all the types of coffee the shop offers and say, "I think I'll splurge today and get an iced latte with two pumps of caramel, thank you. And a blueberry scone heated with butter."

She takes my money and gets to work assembling my order as I look around the shop for what table I want. One in the very back near the bookcase filled with books nobody's ever read looks perfect. I take my seat and wait for my order to be ready, happy I made this decision to forgo all that cleaning up after the girls until later.

Or maybe Connor will come back and see it needs to be done, so he'll take care of that business.

The thought barely enters my head before I roll my eyes. Of course, he won't clean up. I can't remember a single occasion when my husband ever did anything like that. He doesn't even put away his clean clothes when I leave them ready for him in a basket on his side of the bed.

Would it be so hard to pitch in once in a while?

"Jamie! Order for Jamie!" the girl behind the counter calls out, and I hurry up to get my coffee and scone.

We exchange pleasantries, and on the way back to my table, the sweet scent of blueberries fills my nose as steam wafts up from the scone. Thanks to my new friend's suggestion, I know this one will be much better than last time.

Eager to dive in to my treat, I break off a piece and pop it into my mouth. Even though it's very moist due to the butter, it's too hot, and I hurriedly take a drink of my iced latte to wash it down. Consumed by trying to stop the scone from burning the roof of my mouth, I don't see Kelsey until she's standing next to my table.

"Let me guess," she says with a chuckle. "It's not as dry as the Sahara, but now it's too hot. I should have mentioned that to you when I told you about the butter trick. I hope you didn't burn your mouth."

I motion to the chair on the other side of the table and nod. "I did, but thankfully, I got myself an iced latte today, so I was able to cool things down nicely. Join me. I'm here celebrating a night off."

My friend's expression tells me she doesn't understand, so when she sits down, I explain myself. "My daughters are at a friend's house having a sleepover, so it's a free night for me."

Kelsey's eyes light up, but that accentuates her scars so she returns to looking like herself quite quickly. "Doesn't that mean you and your husband can have a night to yourselves? I have to imagine having two young daughters means you don't get many nights like that."

I don't want to show her how unlikely that is and how unhappy I am about that fact, but it's impossible for me to keep how I feel a secret. My mother used to say I never had an emotion that didn't cross my face, and although I've had to get much better controlling my expressions since dealing with all the mothers at gymnastics, I doubt I could hide my disgust with Connor at this moment.

Still, I can't go raving about my husband's behavior since no one wants that, so I force a smile and answer her question. "Maybe, but Connor has a lot on his plate these days. He's probably going to be busy with work tonight."

Instinctively, I watch her face for any clue to what she feels about that. I've learned dealing with all the mothers at gymnastics that what people truly think isn't always clear by what they say. No, the truth is usually found in a person's expression.

I don't see any reaction from Kelsey, which I hope means she doesn't pity me. Of all the things people can feel about me, pity is the worst. I've seen it on the faces of some of the mothers when they look at Maris, and I just don't think I could deal with anyone feeling that way about me.

"Well, it's still nice to have some time to yourself, right?" she asks before brushing a crumb off her pale blue T-shirt that's very flattering on her.

I consider mentioning how much I like that shirt on her, but I'm not sure we're at that place in our friendship, so I simply answer her question. "It is. So for the next hour, I'm going to sit here and relax. After that, I'm not sure what I want to do. I have to admit that's a nice thing, though. Most days, every moment is planned out with activities and chores I have to get out of the way."

She turns around to face the board and then looks back at me. "I think you've got the right idea with that iced latte and scone. I'll be right back. Do you need anything while I'm up there?"

I shake my head and shrug. "I'm good."

While Kelsey is gone to the counter, all I can think is

those two words are the biggest lie I've ever told. I'm not anywhere close to good.

In fact, I think my life may just be what I've always feared. I think it's just like all the other mothers' lives.

And I have no idea how to change that.

CHAPTER FIVE

onnor

BRYAN IS WAITING FOR ME WHEN I PARK MY CAR AT THE community center. Dressed in tan pants that aren't wrinkled and a light green T-shirt, he looks like a hiker. Or maybe it's the perpetual tan he always seems to have and the way his light brown hair looks like he just ran his fingers through it and left the house. He only lives a few blocks away from me, so we should spend more time together. I guess that would require me listing him as something more personal than Guy From Work in my contacts.

"Hey! Ready for some great hiking?" he calls out as I slam my car door shut.

I'm ready for anything that doesn't involve dealing with my wife or eight screaming girls.

"Sure!" I say in a forced tone of enthusiasm.

It's not that I don't want to go hiking. That's as good a way to spend my afternoon as any other. As long as it keeps me away from my house, I'm fine. It's just in the big scheme of things, hiking isn't exactly top on my list of ways to occupy myself on a beautiful sunny day off from work.

When I reach Bryan, exuberance is practically radiating off him. I guess he really likes hiking.

Taking a page out of my wife's social climbing book, I figure I'll get to know him a bit more today and see how that can help me at work. He's the new favorite of our boss, so it can't hurt.

"I figured we'd walk the paths that surround the community. They aren't tough by any means, but they'll give us a nice workout and we'll get a ton of fresh air. Sound good?"

With a nod, I agree to his plans, and we set off across the parking lot to where the woods meet the grounds here at the community center. Bryan breezily chats about how the weather is perfect for us to be out on the trails today, not really stopping to hear my opinion as he moves from that topic to something about a news story he read this morning at breakfast. Normally, I'd find that rude, but today I don't feel like participating in much chit chat, so I'm okay with him monopolizing the conversation.

Ten minutes into our hike, we haven't seen another soul on the trail, which seems odd to me since weekends are usually busy around here. It's a beautiful Saturday afternoon. I can't believe more people didn't have the same idea Bryan had.

"Where is everybody?" I ask when he takes a break from talking as we climb a small hill.

He laughs at that question and points toward a clearing a few yard away. "Maybe up there. I'd think it would be more crowded out here today."

"Me too. The sun's shining, the weather's not too hot, and it's the weekend."

Our conversation goes nowhere rather quickly. Maybe it would be better if I let him talk more for a while until I think of something interesting to discuss. The last thing I want is him telling Martin at work while he's in his office yucking it up like he does every day at lunch that I'm a huge bore. That won't help me get that promotion I've been hoping to get this year.

We reach the clearing and find no one there. How odd. Maybe everyone is out on the golf course. They did say all tee times were booked for this weekend.

"Hmmph, I thought there would be someone up here," Bryan says like he's disappointed.

Maybe I am a huge bore. Damn! I need to get some conversation going, or I'm going to blow this opportunity to brown nose the boss's favorite.

"I think they're all on the golf course. I tried to book a tee time, and they were booked solid this weekend and next."

That seems to interest Bryan, and he turns around to face me like I've finally uttered something that didn't bore him to tears. "Oh, yeah. That's right. Martin wanted the two of us to play a round of golf tomorrow, but no go. The only place in town that had any spots open was the municipal course, but you know how that one is. I swear they never even ask people to replace their divots, and it's obvious no one really takes care of the course. It's like golfing on a road filled with potholes every time I've tried there."

This is my chance. He brought up work and our boss, so all I have to do is keep the topic alive by saying something interesting.

Except my mind is utterly and completely fucking blank. Son of a bitch! I just need one thing to add to the conversation, and I have nothing. I'm blowing this opportunity. I need to fix this right now!

Desperate to say something, I blurt out, "That Martin is a great golfer, isn't he? I've seen him on the course when I'm playing, and he's definitely a cut above."

By the time I finish speaking, I'm filled with dread. Yes, I kept the conversation going, but I made it seem like Martin and I aren't anywhere close to the same level, socially or when it comes to golf.

Bryan shrugs, so I quickly add, "I made sure to tell him that when we talked after we finished and were hanging out in the clubhouse."

At least that makes it sound like my boss doesn't shun me like some social leper he can't stand being around outside of work.

I wait for some response from my hiking partner, but he seems more interested in something rustling in the bushes. Making his way over to where I imagine an animal is doing its private business, he points at the shrub and mouths, "Look at this!"

Look at what? A gopher taking a shit? How the hell is this guy the new office favorite?

Playing along, I follow him and stop a few feet away from the bush, just in case it's some far more vicious animal than what I'm imagining. As I take my place next to Bryan, I whisper, "It might be something that doesn't appreciate humans interfering in its alone time."

He turns to look at me and smiles before he whispers, "You know, you're way funnier outside the office. I didn't know that about you."

Okay, that sounds good. He can certainly feel free to report that back to Martin. Everyone loves a guy who's got a great sense of humor. I never saw myself as that kind of person, but hey, if he thinks so, that's fine with me.

Whatever makes our boss think more highly of me so he wants to give me that raise later this year works for me.

A noise behind us startles me, so I pull my gun out. There's nobody there, though.

I open my mouth to thank him for the compliment, but just then, he sees the gun. "Hey, let me see that. I didn't realize you owned a gun. Damn, Connor. You're way cooler than I thought."

He grabs it from my hold, so I quickly say, "Bryan, be careful with that. Do you know anything about guns?"

But his attention seems fixed on that poor creature in the weeds. "Check it out. Let's see how this hedgehog does when it's running for its life," Bryan says with a laugh.

Before I can say he shouldn't shoot at anything, he takes aim at the animal and misses. Great. Now we can continue our walk.

"Oh, well. Maybe next time," I mumble as I reach for the gun.

But he's not ready to go just yet.

Taking aim for a second time, he shoots at something, although I can't imagine it's still that animal from before. He's not stupid enough to stick around when someone's trying to kill him.

"Son of a bitch! Almost got him!" Bryan calls out.

So he's a liar who has a gun fetish. Good to know. How is this guy a favorite of my boss? Martin has always been a pretty serious person. I have a hard time understanding how this guy's clown act works on our boss.

"Come on," I say, hating how I sound almost like I'm pleading. "Give me the gun back, and let's keep going. I'm sure we'll see more animals along the path up here."

But Bryan isn't persuaded. Waving the gun around, he laughs. "Take it easy, Connor. You're so tight someone could stick a piece of coal up your ass and there'd be a diamond in no time."

As I try to think of something clever to say back to him, he brags about how he owns a gun with some capability I know nothing about. I'm truly questioning how this guy is the star in my boss's eyes. Does he have dirt on him? He must because it's not like his personality is anything great.

Just then, I hear the gun go off, and I spin around to see Bryan on the ground. One glance at his chest shows me he fucking shot himself.

With my gun!

Looking around for anyone to help me, I see not a single soul. Where the hell is everyone today? This path should be packed with my neighbors on a day like this.

I stare down at him lying in the dirt and notice a huge

rock next to his head. He's lucky he didn't bash his skull when he fell.

"Bryan?" I say, unsure what's happening right now.

Christ, he isn't dead, is he? That's all I need today.

Crouching down beside him, I shake him by the shoulder but he doesn't move. He just continues to stare up at nothing.

"Bryan, man. You have to get up. Talk to me. Are you okay?" I ask as my gaze scans his body before coming to rest at the spot where the bullet entered just around his ribs.

For a few seconds, I watch for any sign he's still breathing. It's like time stops as I stare at his chest, but then finally, he inhales. Thank God!

I check my pocket and realize I didn't bring my cell phone. Fuck! The one day I need the damn thing and I don't have it. I blame Jamie. If she hadn't made my pants a wrinkled mess, I would have remembered my phone and an ambulance would be on its way right now.

"Bryan, don't worry man. I'll be right back. I'm going to go get help. Hang on, man. I'm just going back down to the community center to call an ambulance."

I run back down the trail to get someone to call 9-1-1. By the time I reach the community center, I'm winded and barely able to get the words out to the cute girl manning the reception desk.

"Call…I need you to call…" I sputter out, but I need to catch my breath before I can get the entire sentence out.

"Are you okay, sir? Should I call an ambulance or something? A man your age should watch out."

I ignore her idiotic remark about my age while I take

a few deep breaths in and then say, "Call 9-1-1! The man I was hiking with on the trail that heads west shot himself. Call now!"

She hurries to do as I demand while I consider what I should do. Should I go back to where Bryan is no doubt lying on the ground in utter agony, or should I stay here and wait for the paramedics so I can show them exactly where he is?

The girl finishes with the dispatcher and hangs up. "They said they'll be here in a few minutes. Are you okay, sir? Do you want me to get you some water or something?" she asks, wide-eyed like she's as terrified as I was a few minutes ago back in the clearing.

I wave off her suggestions and shake my head. "I'm fine. I just needed to catch my breath. Why aren't they here yet? Don't we have a dedicated ambulance corps for this community? They should be here by now, shouldn't they?"

She doesn't answer but simply nods. A lot of good she is in a crisis. And these are the people we supposedly pay to help us? Thank God I'm not bleeding profusely or something equally as terrible. God knows if I'd be alive by the time the paramedics arrived.

Instead of waiting with her, I walk outside and begin pacing back and forth in front of the entrance to the building. Jesus Christ, what is taking these people so long? Do they answer all emergency calls like this? The guy could be dead up there by now.

I stop as that thought fills my head. I barely know Bryan, and what I do know about him isn't great, especially the part about him being my boss's new favorite for some reason no one knows but the two of them. That aside, I don't want to see him die.

Finally, I hear the sirens and see the flashing lights as the ambulance pulls into the parking lot. The driver and his partner jump out and run toward me as I try to remember everything that happened.

"Who called for an ambulance?" the woman from the passenger side asks.

I point toward the trail and say, "I did. Follow me. He's up on the hill. He was waving a gun around and..."

The driver looks over at his partner and then at me as I try to find the right words to explain what happened. "And what?"

"He shot himself."

For some reason, they look around the parking lot. Are they waiting for someone else? Why aren't we hurrying up the path to help Bryan?

"Are you saying someone brought a gun on the hiking path? Did he shoot it? This is a pretty residential area, sir."

Already tired of these two, I try to keep my cool as I say, "Yes, he shot it. He was trying to kill some animal. Then he was waving it around, and it went off. Just follow me, okay? You'll see."

As they hurry to keep up with me while I race along the trail, the woman calls out, "Perhaps we should get the police involved?"

I turn around and glare at the two of them. "There's a person up here hurt. Call whoever you want, but he needs you two now!"

My anger soars inside me, and I swear at the next community board meeting, I'm going to bring up how ineffective these people are. We pay for this community to be safe. Clearly, we aren't getting our money's worth with these two.

The three of us reach the clearing, and I stop dead at the sight of Bryan all bloody lying on the ground. He isn't moving, and when I zero in on his chest, he's still.

Oh my God! He can't be dead. I still can't figure out how he shot himself. What kind of moron doesn't understand to keep guns away from your damn body?

The two paramedics quickly jump into action, and as they hover over Bryan trying to save his life, it's obvious it's a useless cause. He's gone.

But none of this makes sense.

For the next ten minutes, I stand there in shock as the man and woman do their job. I hear him make a call to the police, but they don't speak to me again. I try to understand what's happened. Nothing works. This is crazy.

When the police arrive, two uniformed officers look down at Bryan's dead body for a few moments before walking around the clearing searching for something.

After five minutes of walking around, they make their way to where I'm standing off to the side so I'm not in the way. My eyes are drawn to their nametags just above their chest pockets. Ramon and Raintree. Sounds like a sitcom someone in Hollywood would dream up. Two cops from different backgrounds get together and fight crime in a suburban Maryland town where on many days the most exciting thing to happen is someone left their garbage cans out at the curb too long and the HOA has to send a threatening letter saying they're going to levy a fine if the receptacles aren't put away properly.

I wouldn't watch it, but I bet lots of people would.

"What is your name, sir?" Officer Ramon asks, and I lift my gaze to look at his face.

He reminds me of that actor my wife thinks is handsome. Actually, what she says is he's hot. He's Hispanic, and she claims there's something about the way he smiles that does it for her. The man in front of me looks a little more weathered than the guy Jamie drools over, but I bet she'd like him. She has a type. Why she wanted to date me makes no sense when I think of that.

"Connor," I answer in a flat voice, still not understanding how any of this happened. "Connor Jennings."

"Okay, Mr. Jennings. And your address?"

I give him my address and then he asks, "You were the person who called this in?" the officer asks as he fishes out a notebook and pen from his shirt pocket.

"Yes. I mean no. I was with Bryan when it happened, but I wasn't the person who called 9-1-1. That was the girl at the community center. I ran down there to get help."

Officer Ramon nods and hums as he jots down the highlights of what I've said so far and then lifts his head to look at me again. "You and the victim, Bryan Corsei, were just out for a hike this afternoon when he was shot? Is that what happened?"

I nod before answering, "Yeah, but he wasn't shot. He shot himself."

That sounds ridiculous, but I don't know how else to say it.

"Did he say he wanted to kill himself?"

I shake my head, unsure how to answer that. Did he?

I don't know. I wasn't exactly listening that closely to what he was saying.

"No. At least I don't think so. It's hard to say."

More humming and nodding happen before he looks me right in the eyes and asks, "Why didn't you just call the ambulance from your cell phone?"

I sheepishly pat the pockets in my pants for some reason, even though I know my phone isn't on me. "I...I guess I don't have it. To be honest, I'm not sure why I didn't realize it before when I was leaving the house, but I don't have my phone."

That's not completely honest, but I'm not really in the mood to explain about how little care my wife takes with my clothes. That information doesn't seem necessary for these two to know.

His gaze trails down my body to where my hands were feeling around for my phone a few seconds ago and then back up to my face. I see immediately he doesn't believe me.

"So I'm guessing you routinely leave your phone at home when you come out here hiking?"

For a split second, I consider lying. It certainly would make things go better at this moment. I should just say I always leave my phone at home when I go out hiking on these trails, but something tells me Officer Ramon wouldn't believe that. I'm a pretty good liar, but I'm not sure I could lie about something right now, and even worse, all he'd have to do is talk to my wife and he'd find out the truth.

"Um, no. Actually, I usually have my phone on me."

Officer Raintree finally speaks up and from behind his fellow policeman, he asks far less politely than his partner, "So then why didn't you have it on you today? That seems odd, doesn't it?"

I scramble to think of an answer that will sound plausible. I don't know why I didn't bring my phone with me when I came to meet Bryan. It's completely unlike me. I always have my phone with me.

Shaking my head, I answer the best I can. "I don't know. I did run into some problems when I was trying to find a pair of pants to wear today. My wife had stuffed them into the back of the closet, and they were wrinkly when I found them. I was pretty angry about that. Maybe that made me forget my phone. I don't know. I imagine it's sitting on the bed where I must have left it before I walked out of the house to come here."

I know how that sounds. Like I'm some idiot. That's why I didn't want to mention it.

"Okay, onto what happened here. So you said he was waving a gun around and then he shot himself?"

Again, I nod. "Yes. Well, there may have been some more conversation between those two things. I don't know. It all happened so fast. We stopped here in the clearing and were talking, and then the next thing I knew, the gun went off and he was lying on the ground."

As Officer Ramon writes down my comments, Officer Raintree stares at me like he thinks I'm the one who shot Bryan. I want to say I would never hurt a soul, but I know I couldn't pull off that lie.

Considering my past, that is.

I watch as the paramedics wheel Bryan away on a stretcher, his entire body and face covered by a white sheet. When I turn my attention back to the two officers standing in front of me, I see them staring at me.

"Can I go now? This has been incredibly upsetting."

"We have a few more questions," Raintree snaps. "Like for example, did you and the victim routinely come out on these trails hiking? Was this a regular thing you two did together?"

"No. In fact, today is the first time we've ever done anything outside of work together."

That seems to interest Officer Ramon, and once he jots down that detail, he asks, "So you two were coworkers? Where?"

"Chesapeake Siding and Garage Doors. We're both salesmen."

"Okay. So while you didn't routinely go hiking together, you two were friends?" Ramon stops for a moment before adding, "Work friends, I mean."

"I guess you could say that. We both work in the siding division of the company. Bryan was newer at the company than I was."

My answers appear to frustrate Officer Raintree, who pipes up with, "So you were coworkers but not friends? Because you two don't sound very close to me. I mean, I work with Officer Ramon here all the time, and we're friends too because we do things outside of work. That doesn't sound like what was going on between you and Mr. Corsei."

Already irritated by these local cops who probably have dreams of being much bigger than they are, I level my gaze on him and say, "There was nothing going on between me and Bryan. We worked at the same company. I had his number in my phone, and when I needed to get away from my house today since my wife and my two daughters have six preteen girls over for a party, I called him and he asked if I wanted to go hiking. That's it. Now I need to go."

I turn to leave and feel a hand squeeze down on my forearm. Looking back at the two officers, I see it's Officer Raintree who thinks he's going to detain me.

"Do you have something else you want to ask me?" I ask, lifting my gaze to meet his.

"We aren't done yet."

"Well, I am. Unless you're going to arrest me for something, although I can't imagine what crime you think I committed, but unless you have cause to arrest me, I'm going home. Goodbye."

He doesn't let go of my arm, so I yank it away from his hold and walk away. If they want to talk to me again, they're going to need to make a damn appointment.

CHAPTER SIX

amie

DEEP IN THOUGHT ABOUT MY LIFE, I DON'T SEE Kelsey sit down across from me until she clears her throat. Quickly, I force a smile and point at her scone.

"Heated with butter?"

She nods before taking a big bite. I watch her truly enjoy the very simple treat and wonder if I ever look that happy.

After washing down the scone with a few sips of her iced latte, she says, "It's the little tricks in life that make it bearable, don't you think?"

When I don't respond, she adds, "You know, like the butter and heating up the scone to make it less dry."

"Oh, yes. Definitely."

Something about the way she said that thing about the life tricks made me think she meant something else. I don't know what, though. Maybe if I knew her better I'd understand.

"Are you okay? You seem distracted today," Kelsey says.

I know I shouldn't say anything about what's on my mind, but it's not like she's part of my social circle, so why not? It's not like she's one of those mothers I see all the time at practice. To them, I wouldn't speak a single syllable about what may be wrong with my life.

This woman, on the other hand, gives me the impression she wouldn't be judgmental like they would. I focus on her scars and think about how she's likely been on the receiving end of countless looks of judgment because of them. That's probably why she seems so understanding.

The problem is, though, I haven't spoken the truth about my life or my marriage for so long that I'm not sure I know how to do it. God forbid any of those mothers I see every day ever found out what Connor and I owe on that house or how little we actually speak to one another these days. I know what they'd do. They'd put that expression each of them has perfected to show their superiority. It's a look of pity, and I'd rather die than see that when they think of me.

I'm not someone to be pitied. I have everything a woman could ever want. A husband who makes good money. A beautiful home that's as lovely as any in our development. Two incredible daughters who excel at everything they try.

There's no reason to pity me. Save that for people

like Maris and that poor child of hers that is likely going to miss making the gymnastics team. They deserve pity, not me.

Kelsey reaches her hand across the table and gently touches my finger. "I know we don't really know each other, but I'm told I'm a good listener. Feel free to take advantage of that. You look like you need to get something off your chest."

As I look into her dark eyes and try not to stare at the scar on the left side of her face that appears very obvious today, I think she could be the only person I could unburden myself to around here. Connor never wants to hear about any problems, and all those mothers who call themselves my friends would use what I say against me.

It would be nice to talk to someone about things.

With a smile, I let out a heavy sigh I've been keeping in for what seems like years. "I have so much, so complaining makes me feel like I'm not being grateful enough for all the good things there are in my life."

Kelsey nods as I talk, and when I finish, she says, "I understand. I can tell you live with gratitude. You can tell people who are selfish a mile away, and I can promise you that's not what I see in you, Jamie."

Relief washes over me. I'd be mortified if I thought people viewed me as a selfish, ungrateful person.

"Thank you. I try. I know there are many people in the world who would give their left arm to have all I have. It feels silly even thinking of complaining."

Again, she nods. "It's okay if you don't feel comfortable telling me about what's on your mind. We barely know each other."

As if my brain has no way of controlling my mouth, I

blurt out, "But that's why I think I want to. I think someone who knows me would be biased. You wouldn't be."

She takes a bite of her scone and then a sip of her latte before she responds. "That's true. That must be why therapists work. They don't know their clients personally, but they want them to be happy."

I smile at her comment. She's right. That's why telling her what's on my mind might be helpful to me. I've never thought I had anything wrong that warranted a therapist, but what harm could it cause telling Kelsey what's bothering me?

For a few moments, I try to decide how to explain what I'm dealing with, but every way I come up with sounds like whining. Finally, I say, "It's just that I don't want to come across as a woman who doesn't see all she has."

That gets me a big, warm smile that instantly makes me feel better. "You don't have to worry about me thinking that about you. Trust me."

A year ago I would've smiled and thanked her without going any further. Today, though, I need to talk to someone about my life right now.

I look around to see if anyone at the nearby tables may be able to hear me, but there's no one close enough, thankfully. Lowering my voice, I decide to simply state what's on my mind.

"It's just that I didn't imagine my life like it's turned out."

Kelsey likely believes I'm being intentionally cryptic. In truth, I'm unsure how to word the real issue I'm dealing with concerning every part of my life.

When she doesn't say anything, I continue, silently praying to God I don't sound like one of those bratty women who complain when they have it all. "It's just that I...maybe I had an idea of what my life would be, and now I have to figure out how to handle the truth that it isn't that at all."

That doesn't add anything to her understanding, so I'm happy when she doesn't stare across the table at me and say, "Cut to the chase already!"

Two women walk into the café, and I hurriedly look over to see if I know them. I breathe a sigh of relief when I realize I don't. Hopefully, they won't sit at any of the tables around us.

I take a deep breath and let it out through my nose in a rush. I want to talk about this. I just have to suck it up and say the words.

Leaning in toward Kelsey, I say in a voice barely above a whisper, "I feel like my entire life is a fraud."

Her dark eyes fill with sympathy, and I can't help but feel better. Even merely saying that single sentence makes me feel like the weight of the world has been lifted from my shoulders.

"Thank you for not thinking I'm a horrible person. Honestly, I think most people would believe I am because I have so much."

She gives me a tiny smile and then asks, "Can I tell you a story?"

"Sure."

Kelsey swallows hard and blows the air out of her mouth before she starts. "I was a teenager when this happened. In hindsight, I guess I should have known better than to believe in my boyfriend, but that's all water under the bridge. I try to remember what we do as eighteen year old girls shouldn't determine our entire lives."

Even more cryptic than what I said, her words intrigue me. I listen with rapt attention, wondering how this may relate to my problems.

"So, I was eighteen and had the world by the tail. I was a beautiful girl. You probably wouldn't be able to tell that looking at me today, but I had high cheekbones and great skin. I don't think I ever even had more than a pimple or two all during my teenage years. I had no problem attracting boys, and I enjoyed dating, never getting too involved so I was tied down."

When she stops, I smile and say, "Smart girl. Teenage girls too often let themselves get sucked into serious relationships before they're ready to handle them."

She holds her hand up and shakes her head. "Save the compliments for later. Trust me. I wasn't smart enough."

Now I'm intrigued. Without taking my eyes off her as she continues to speak, I lift the iced latte cup to my mouth and take a sip.

"So, it's fall and my friend and I are hanging out downtown in the city we lived in. Actually, it was closer to a small town, but to us, it was our stomping grounds. We're out on a Friday night just having a good time when these three boys approach us at a little store and ask if we want to have some fun. They seemed nice, so we said yes. It all felt very normal since we routinely met new people and hung out with them every weekend."

I sense a sadness has crept into her words, but she

continues to smile as she speaks. I'm curious to know if this story will tell me what happened to give her those terrible scars on her face, but I fear that will be a very dark story, and we likely haven't spoken long enough for her to share that.

"We used to do the same thing where I lived," I say. "It was what you did before the internet when you lived in a small town."

Kelsey nods and then chuckles a little. "True. Life was very different back then. We didn't have phones in our pockets all the time. Meeting people in person was the way it was. So my friend and I met these three guys, and before I say any more, please know that she and I talked about how safe it was for two girls and three guys to be hanging out in the woods together. We weren't stupid. I'd say we were just naïve."

"Things were different back then. Trust me, I know. I wouldn't be happy if my two girls went out with three boys, though. That probably sounds paranoid. Maybe it's just different when you become a mother."

"Hmm…maybe," she says before continuing. "So one of the boys was too drunk to even do much more than talk, so when the five of us met up in the woods near the store, it was basically even—two boys and two girls. My friend wasn't worried, but I had been, so when I saw him fall over a log and his friends said he was just drunk, I felt better about everything."

She stops and then says, "I shouldn't have."

The way she says that is so serious that I feel a chill run down my spine. I'm completely focused on her now, so curious about what could have happened to her.

I wait as she finishes her scone and then washes it down with a big swig of her latte. "So we were hanging out having a good time. It was the same as any other weekend with any other new people. We had a couple beers, laughed a lot, especially at their friend who had passed out in the damp leaves next to the log, and although my friend and I didn't do it, the two boys smoked a joint. When I say it was a very typical night in the town we lived in, I mean it. I think you could have found dozens of us spread throughout the woods that night doing the same exact thing."

My parents were stricter than I imagine hers were, so even at eighteen, I spent very little time with boys. My mother always worried that I'd get pregnant before I married, so she made it her life's work to keep me as pure as possible.

I've always thought I missed out on so many fun times, but now as Kelsey tells me her story, I wonder if my mother had done me the biggest favor. I don't resent her for how closely she watched me back then. Not anymore.

Kelsey looks around the café and then returns her attention to me as a man walks by us before choosing a table on the other side of the room. "So we were having fun, and my friend wanted to be alone with the boy she liked. I don't remember his name, but it doesn't matter. He turned out to be an okay guy. I wish I could say the one I was talking to was."

Now I definitely see she's sadder than when she began telling me her story, so I say, "If you don't want to continue, that's okay. This sounds like a story that comes with a lot of emotion."

"It does, but I think you should hear it. It might give you some perspective on what you're dealing with."

The girl at the counter yells out an order, and one of the women who walked in a few minutes ago grabs two coffees and a hot ham and cheese sandwich to take back to the table she's sharing with her friend near the window. The scent of the ham drifts over toward where we're sitting, and I consider telling Kelsey I'm going to order one, but I don't want to interrupt her story.

"We walked a little further into the woods and got cozy on a couple rocks. Like most boys his age, he was interested in going as far as he could, but I kept him to just kissing. He didn't have an issue with that, which was nice. I knew my friend and the boy she was with weren't too far away, and it was all good. We kissed for a little while and then went to find them."

Kelsey stops, and I swear I see her eyes get teary. I don't want to pressure her to continue if she's upset, but now I'm dying to know what happened.

"Are you okay?" I ask just as I know I should, even if I'm hoping she says yes and keep talking.

Nodding, she says, "It's hard sometimes, but I think this is important."

"Okay. Take your time. I have hours since my girls are having a sleepover at one of their friend's houses."

She doesn't speak for what feels like forever, but it's probably just a few minutes. Feeling awkward, I focus on the last piece of my scone and my latte, which is no longer iced and tastes more like watered down coffee.

When she speaks again, she looks like a different person. More serious. Almost angry.

"Sorry, this always turns hard for me when I get to the part that's more important than the rest of the night."

I want to tell her I'm sorry because she's clearly upset by what she wants to tell me. If I wasn't so interested in hearing it, I'd tell her to feel free to stop, but I have a feeling the rest of the story is going to be important.

Clearing her throat, she says, "We were just kids. All we wanted to do was have a little fun. I thought the guy I was with was okay. We weren't going to spend the rest of our lives together, but what's one night in the woods hanging out and drinking? If only it had been just that."

She stops and then says, "I don't mean to drag things out. I've never been very good at telling this story, but I have the sense you need to hear it. So here's the rest. He didn't rape me or anything terrible like that. He didn't even try much. No, the problem was he had a terrible temper, and when an old busybody man walking through the woods saw us, he told us we needed to leave the area. He wasn't bothering us really. He was just an old man. But that night, he opened his mouth to the wrong person."

I'm practically leaning over the table to hear her as she speaks. I can't be sure, but I have the sense what happened next to her that night explains those horrible scars.

"He went nuts. He chased that poor old man down and beat the hell out of him. I don't know why. I'd never seen anyone drink and get high act like that before. Then after he attacked him, he turned on me. I know you've noticed the scars on my face. Those are from him. So is the one on my abdomen."

Kelsey lifts her blue shirt up just high enough for me

to see a raised scar on her pale skin. "Nice, huh? Thanks to him, I can never have children."

My mouth drops open, and I shake my head at how horrible that must have been for her. "I'm so sorry, Kelsey. He paid for what he did to you and that man, didn't he?"

Sniffling her tears away, she answers, "No. He's never even been questioned."

Horrified at the injustice I'm hearing about, I ask, "Why? How could the authorities let him get away with it?"

She draws her eyebrows in toward her nose and frowns. "He beat me so savagely that night that I ended up in a coma for over a week. By the time I came out of it, I couldn't say for sure what happened. It was only when I went home and my friend felt I could handle the truth that she told me. By that time, all I wanted to do was forget what he did. I didn't want to risk him coming after me again."

I reach across the table and rest my hand on hers. "I'm so sorry. You didn't deserve that, and he deserves to pay for what he did."

"Thank you, Jamie. I wanted to tell you that story because I think it can help you see things about your own life a little more clearly."

Hanging my head, I say, "I feel so stupid right now. You and other people have real issues, and here I am complaining because my oh-so-perfect life isn't as perfect as I dreamed it would be. Thank you for helping me get some perspective."

"Just remember this, Jamie. No matter what happens, you can go on. I did. It's hard. Some days I didn't want to get out of bed. I did, though, and every day things get a little easier for me."

I really have been silly. Sure, I wish Connor would do more things with me and the girls. And yes, I wish our life had more happiness and less stress.

But the big picture is so much better than many people's, and for that, I am thankful.

CHAPTER SEVEN

onnor

JAMIE AND THE GIRLS AREN'T AT HOME WHEN I
return, thank God, so I hurry upstairs to get changed
and look for my damn phone. It's not on the bed, like I
thought it would be, though.

I quickly slip into my shorts and a clean T-shirt and
hurry downstairs to search there. I swear if Jamie moved
my phone I'm going to lose it. I tell her all the time to just
let it be. Time and again, I've warned her not to touch
my cell. Does this woman even listen when I say things
to her?

Thankfully, she keeps the house spotless, which only
seems right since she's here all day while I work and the
girls are at school. What else does she have to do with
her time?

Tossing cushions off the sofa, I jam my hands down

into the back of the piece of furniture and feel around. Nothing. I turn to the chair next, but it's not there either.

Maybe in the kitchen.

I hurry in there and scan the room in front of me, but I don't see it. The kitchen isn't spotless, so that makes my search ten times more difficult. Pushing aside bags of chips and pretzels Jamie has left on the counter, I look through every inch of the kitchen and find nothing.

Where the hell is my phone?

Panic rushes through me. I don't keep anything illegal on my phone, but it's not exactly something I want anyone to scroll through. Phones are personal. The last thing I want is someone looking through it without some context.

I run back upstairs and frantically begin searching around the bedroom. My wife insists on having furniture that's all up off the floor. She claims it looks more refined. Right now, all it's doing is making my job finding my phone harder than it needs to be.

Crawling around on my hands and knees, I run my palms over the carpeting but feel nothing. This isn't possible. Phones don't just grow legs and walk away. It has to be here somewhere. I flip up the bedspread and search under the bed, and there about a foot in I feel my phone.

How on earth did it get there?

I pull it out and look at it in my hand. With a swipe across the screen, I get to my home page and see no new calls or messages. I should call my boss and tell him about Bryan. Jesus, how the hell am I going to phrase that news?

After thinking of that awfulness, I sit down on the

floor next to the bed and lean my head back against the mattress. I can't believe what's happened. Bryan is dead from some freak accident that I guess is technically considered suicide. Christ, what kind of unlucky break was that? I can't imagine what he was thinking shooting a goddamned gun on a hike over the trails around our development. It's a suburban area, for God's sake. What if he had mistakenly hurt a child?

The worst part of it is he did it with my gun. I didn't offer that information, but it's only a matter of time before the police find out. Even those two bumbling idiots Ramon and Raintree will figure that out. Then what will happen? They can't blame me. My prints aren't even on the gun since I didn't even hold it after slipping it into my pants.

Son of a bitch! Who the hell am I kidding? Of course, my fingerprints are all over that gun. It's mine, for Christ's sake! As soon as they know, those two cops are going to zero in on me as the one who killed Bryan.

Staring down at my phone, I try to find the right words to say to my boss, but I've got nothing. Maybe Bryan's wife will call Martin. He was married, wasn't he? I don't know. We weren't that close. He might have mentioned having a wife once or twice, didn't he?

As I sit there trying to catalog all the things I know about Bryan Corsei, I quickly realize I knew next to nothing about him. I know where he worked and what he did. I know he came to work at Chesapeake Siding and Garage Doors a few months ago. And I know he lived in the same community I do. That's about it. Until this afternoon, we'd never done anything outside of work. Hell, we rarely did anything together during working hours since he was the boss's favorite and Martin routinely rewarded him with much better leads than the rest of us.

I better not keep thinking like that, or it might slip out at some point, and I'll sound like some jealous asshole. The guy's dead. No need to bring up that he was the office favorite.

Footsteps tear me out of my thoughts, and a second later, my wife appears in the doorway to the bedroom looking downright disturbed. Probably something with the little darlings. I wonder where they all went. Not that I'm unhappy they're gone, but something tells me I won't be getting any peace tonight, nevertheless.

She stares down at me in horror, like I've done something wrong, so I brace myself for some complaint that will likely have me running back to the damn grocery store. So much for a leisurely weekend off. I swear those kids with their social schedule are really starting to cramp my style.

"Oh my God! Connor! Did you hear about that man who got killed on one of the hiking paths? I heard about it when I was at the café having an iced latte. Some woman came in and told everyone just as I was walking out. They're saying someone attacked him. I can't believe it!"

So the news has started to spread. Great.

"Believe it. I was there."

I stand up after saying that, needing to get on with this day. Jamie shakes her head as her mouth hangs open in shock.

"It was Bryan, one of my coworkers. He and I were out on a hike, and he shot himself by mistake. I ran to get help, but by the time I got back with the paramedics, it was too late."

"Did you see the person who did it? Oh, God, I hope the police catch him quickly. This is terrible."

I squint at her, having a hard time not blowing up in her face at her idiocy. The woman never listens. She gets something into that head of hers, and dammit if any facts can penetrate whatever delusion she's decided to believe today.

"Try listening, Jamie. Not someone. There's no one to catch. He shot himself. It was a mistake. He was waving the gun around and accidentally shot himself."

My wife's eyes get as big as saucers. "Shot himself? You mean like suicide?"

Shaking my head, I let out a heavy sigh. If my own wife doesn't believe it, I can't imagine how hard it's going to be telling my boss that story.

I pinch the bridge of my nose as a headache begins forming behind my eyes. "Yes, like suicide. Exactly like it, in fact, since he shot himself, Jamie!"

"Why would he want to kill himself on the nature path in the neighborhood? That doesn't seem right. And why would he chose to do it in front of you? Don't people who commit suicide usually do that alone?" my wife asks, only making my situation worse.

Already bored with this conversation, I sigh again. Jamie looks at me like I'm going to answer her question with anything but the actual answer. Sorry to disappoint her.

"I don't know. It's not like I asked him to join me and kill himself."

I begin walking toward the bathroom to escape her,

but she follows me, continuing to talk. "I don't understand this, Connor. I can't imagine anyone has ever killed themselves up on that path."

Then, of course, she has to make it about the girls.

"Oh, God. What are the other mothers going to think when they find out our daughters' father was with someone who committed suicide right here in the neighborhood?"

Unable to stop myself from answering that inane question, I turn around and glare at her. "What the hell does that matter? Why would they think anything? I had nothing to do with his death."

"Well, I don't want the mothers to think badly of the girls. That's all I was saying. I don't think our daughters should suffer because of something that happened to you."

"Whatever. I'm sure they'll be gossiping about someone else soon enough."

I don't wait for her response before walking into the bathroom and shutting the door behind me. Maybe I'll take another shower. I barely did anything since my first one this morning, but after what happened on the trail, I feel like I need to restart this day.

For the next ten minutes, I scrub my body in a desperate attempt to cleanse myself of every last trace of what happened today. Leave it to Bryan to completely screw up a nice hike. Asshole.

Nearly ready to get out of the shower and restart my day, a terrible thought pushes out every other one in my brain. He killed himself with my gun. I have no way of explaining that.

Once those cops figure that out, they're going to focus entirely on me.

Thinking back on Ramon and Raintree, I know what's going to happen. Those two couldn't solve a crime if the answer was tattooed on their brains. The second they find out it's my gun Bryan shot himself with, they're going to be looking at me for this, even though it was an accident.

Son of a bitch. This is what I get for wanting to be better friends with people at work.

CHAPTER EIGHT

amie

My mind races as I stand in the middle of the bedroom I share with my husband trying to digest the terrible news he just told me. Someone killed themselves on the nature path. It's so hard to believe. This is why I always tell Connor to keep his guns locked up tightly. If the girls ever got their hands on one of those things, I don't want to think about what may happen.

Thankfully, my phone rings, tearing me away from those terrible thoughts. I see it's Maris and immediately answer, just in case something's happened to one of the girls.

"Hey, Maris! What's up? Is everything okay?" I ask as I start to pace across the bedroom floor.

"The girls are fine. I just wanted to know if you heard

about that shooting that took place up on the trails. Five minutes ago, Alita called me to say she heard someone got shot up there. Have you or Connor heard anything about it?"

Oh, God. This is my worst nightmare come true. After all I've done to make sure Cassandra and Danielle are as popular as possible, all of my diligent work is about to be undone by one stupid thing. When everyone hears Connor was with that guy, they're going to take it out on my girls.

I have to choose my words carefully here. Maris isn't the type of person to immediately decide Connor's guilty, but I need to lay the groundwork for any ugliness that may come later from some of the other mothers.

Forcing myself to smile and hoping I sound as casual and lighthearted as I usually do, I answer, "I heard about it at the coffee shop. It's a terrible accident, I hear. The man didn't mean to shoot anyone. He just made a mistake, I think."

Maris lets out an audible sigh of relief. "Oh, thank God. I was worried we had a hardened criminal in our midst for a few seconds there. I knew you'd have the dirt, Jamie. Thanks so much for clearing that up. I feel like I can let the girls go back outside to enjoy the pool now that I know we don't have a gun-wielding maniac running around."

"Absolutely! I think it's just a tragic mistake all around. I'm glad you were looking out for my girls, though. Thank you for that."

"Oh, it's my pleasure. Your daughters are practically angels, so it's always great to have them stay over. I'll let you go enjoy your night off from being a mom. Do you and Connor have anything special planned? Maybe a candlelight dinner or going out to a nice restaurant?"

I wish. Knowing my husband, he's going to sit and stew about what happened up on that path all night. The best I can hope for is ordering in a pizza from that new place in town.

She can't know that, though, so I have to lie.

"Oh, I don't know. Between you and me, I think that husband of mine is planning something special because he's been dropping hints all day. I'll be sure to give you all the details tomorrow morning, if I'm not hungover, or Monday when I drop the girls off at practice."

Maris sounds genuinely excited for my surprise and says, "Oh, that's great! Enjoy yourselves tonight. I know how few and far between nights out can be when you have two kids. Don't worry about Cassandra and Danielle. They'll be fine here. We're ordering pizza from Nico's and making ice cream sundaes tonight. I know they should be watching what they're eating because of gymnastics and the big meet coming up, but they'll burn off all those calories, don't worry."

As much as I know I should be concerned with my daughters' calorie intake, they've already made the team, so it'll be fine. It's Tiffanie who should be watching what she eats. She still hasn't made the team, and if she doesn't get that vault down pat, the only thing she's going to have to make her happy is that pizza and ice cream.

"Thanks so much, Maris. You guys have fun tonight. I'll be over to pick the girls up right around eleven tomorrow. Sound good?"

"That sounds perfect! Enjoy your night off tonight. You deserve it!"

I end the call and sit down on the edge of the bed. I can feel a headache starting because of all this craziness. Connor knows how hard I've worked to make sure the girls are successful and popular. Does he understand this one instance could upend all I've done? Then what are we going to do?

No, I can't think like that! I've worked too damn long to have all I've achieved to go up in smoke over someone else's mistake.

I need to get ahead of this right now. There's no way I'm letting the rumor mill get a hold of this story without my controlling it. But how?

Let's think. That guy obviously had some deep-seated mental problems. He must have to shoot himself. Then again, Connor said it was an accident, so maybe he wasn't intending on killing himself.

That's even better. I can work with an accident. I just need to know the man's name, and then I can get to work containing this mess.

I hurry over to the bathroom door and knock on it. "Connor! Are you finished in the shower yet? I need to ask you a question."

Nothing but silence.

Ordinarily, I'd wait and give him some privacy, but there's no time for that now. Flinging the door open, I walk into the bathroom and hear the shower still running. Strange. My husband isn't normally one for long, luxurious showers.

"Are you okay in there?" I ask before swiping my hand across the mirror to clear away the steam.

Behind the glass door, Connor says, "Since you can

hear the water still running, I must be in here. Sometimes I wonder about you, Jamie."

He really can be quite testy sometimes. Whatever. I'm not interested in having that conversation with him right now.

"Connor, what was the name of the man who got shot today?"

Making a low sound like a growl, he answers, "He didn't get shot, Jamie. He shot himself. Try phrasing it correctly."

"Fine. What was the man's name who shot himself up on the path today?"

My husband doesn't respond, so after nearly half a minute, I ask, "Did you hear me? I need the man's name, Connor!"

Just then, the door to the shower flies open toward me, and out steps Connor, dripping wet and reaching for the towel. The look on his face says he's not happy with my questions, but if he knew what I needed to know for, he'd understand how important this is to our family.

"I don't ask for much, Jamie. I just want some peace and quiet, and I expect that when I come in here to take a shower, I'll at least have a few minutes to myself," he says gruffly as he begins to dry off.

"Fine, Connor. I'm not here to interrupt anything. Just tell me the man's name, and I'll be gone."

My husband complains about not having any space of his own in a house filled with women instead of answering my one simple question. I swear this man makes me so mad!

Disgusted by his unwillingness to help me, I yell,

"Just tell me the goddamned man's name, will you? Give me the name, and I'll leave you alone, okay?"

My screaming stuns him for a few seconds, and the two of us stand just a few feet apart looking at one another like neither of us knows what to say. Why does he have to make everything so damn difficult?

He finishes drying off, so I ask once more, "What was the man's name who shot himself today?"

It's not an outlandish question. I don't know why he has to give me a hard time instead of simply answering me.

Connor sighs and answers, "Bryan Corsei. That was his name. Happy now?"

I can't stop myself from rolling my eyes as I push past him on my way out of the bathroom. Happy? No, dearest husband, I'm not happy. I'm tired of dealing with you being miserable, and now it looks like all I've done to make sure our daughters get the best chance in this world is going to be ruined because of your stupid walking pal shooting himself.

So, no, on the whole, I'm not happy, Connor.

If I thought it would be worth the time and effort necessary to say all of that to him, I would, but I know Connor Jennings better than that. He'd just complain that I'm nagging again, and then he'd either storm out or we'd have a fight.

Definitely not the way I had hoped to spend a night without our girls.

Armed with at least the man's name, now I can get to work. I have to do this right. It would be easier to start with one of the nicer mothers like Maris, but while that would be less painful, I know I have to call the biggest, baddest mother at gymnastics.

Vanessa Dennis.

Like all the other mothers, I usually refer to her by her initials behind her back. VD. It's childish, but the woman is as awful as a venereal disease.

Vanessa Dennis is mean and intentionally cruel to anyone she doesn't like, and her distaste for someone doesn't even have to be something serious. She once insisted everyone blackball Janine Matthews and her daughter because Janine didn't have the time to buy a candy bar Allie Dennis was selling for cheerleading. For three months, poor Janine got no invitations to join any of us for coffee after practice or the daily walk many of us used to take, and her daughter didn't get to sleep over at any of the girls' homes because no one asked her in fear that if they did, then Vanessa would make them a target for her wrath.

My hands shake as I scroll through my contacts list. When I stop on Vanessa's name, I groan. Never once have I spoken to that woman without being miserable when the call is over. I can be catty, but she's downright awful.

It doesn't matter. All I have to do is plant the seed in her mind that Connor had nothing to do with what happened and everything will be fine.

After taking a deep breath and letting it out until there's no air left in my lungs, I press call and try to keep calm, even as my heart races. Vanessa very quickly answers, which seems like a good sign, and I carefully listen to her voice. She sounds chipper enough.

"Hey, Jamie. What's up? I saw your husband at the

grocery store this morning before I brought Allie over to your house. He looked almost sick. Is everything okay?"

That's her style. It seems innocuous and possibly like she's full of concern for Connor's health, but I know her too well. That little comment was meant to make me apologize for something he did. It was likely nothing important, like he didn't say hello when she saw him, but I'll do what I have to in order to get moving on to what I want to say.

"Oh, you know how men are. They get so cranky when you ask them to run to the store for you. He didn't mention seeing you, so that's why he didn't say hi, I'm sure. Connor was just unhappy he couldn't sit around and watch golf instead of doing me one, tiny favor."

She has a habit of humming as people speak, something I've always found irritating, and today she's so loud she almost drowns out my very words. Like with everything else she does, it's always to make sure she's in total control of the situation.

"Oh, well that explains it. I thought he was just being rude. I couldn't imagine what I may have done to upset him. I even asked my husband, but John didn't know what could be wrong."

I'd bet a hundred dollars not a single word of that was a lie. I can see her sitting down with her husband to discuss why Connor didn't speak to her at the grocery store. Sometimes she can be so ridiculous. Her husband, on the other hand, likely stared at her with his trademark look of disinterest he seems to wear every time I see him. John Dennis rarely says anything whenever he's around all of us, but I've always had the sense his indifference isn't only what he feels when he's in public with the other gymnastics parents.

There's no time to focus on that now, though. I've got more important things to take care of today with her.

I have to phrase things just right, or this phone call will all be for nothing.

"Believe it or not, things actually got much worse for my poor husband after he had to run to the store for me. He and this man he knows from his work decided to enjoy the beautiful weather and take a hike along the paths around the area. I don't know what exactly happened, but the man took out a gun and began shooting at small animals. Then, and I have no idea why, he turned the gun on himself! Connor was mortified and ran to get help from the community center."

Vanessa doesn't say a word for a long moment, and every second I hear silence on the phone is a second I'm sure I've blown my chance to save the girls from any backlash that may come from what happened on the hiking path today. I'm almost eager enough to continue talking, but thankfully, she finally starts speaking.

"Oh, my God! I heard something about a shooting, but I had no idea someone shot themselves. Even if it's an accident, that's terrible. How is Connor holding up? I can only imagine how awful it must be to see someone shoot themselves."

Good. She sounds upset and worried, just as I hoped she would. Now to finish this off.

"He's okay, but he's terribly upset. It's not everyday someone shoots themselves in front of you. God, that poor man. He must have been dealing with some terrible demons. Connor's relaxing now, and I hope I can get him to talk about it later. I just don't think it's healthy to keep things like that all bottled up inside."

"That's a good idea. I imagine he's very bothered after that. I know I would be. By the way, Allie had a great time at the party today. She'd love to have your daughters over for a sleepover next week. Sound good?"

Holy shit! This has turned out even better than I ever thought it could. I got to tell her about Connor and made it clear that he had nothing to do with that man's death, and now she wants to have the girls over next weekend.

"Oh, that would be wonderful! I'm sure Cassandra and Danielle will be thrilled. I'll be sure to tell them when they get home. I better go now. Connor just got out of the shower, so I'm hoping to make him some dinner and see if we can talk about what he went through today. No good keeping it to himself, you know?"

She chuckles for some reason and says, "Oh, definitely. Well, I'll see you Monday at drop off. Tell Connor we hope he's going to be okay."

"Thanks, Vanessa! See you at drop off!" I chirp out, happier than I thought I could be this afternoon.

At least I was able to handle that. Now I just have to deal with that husband of mine.

And to think I was planning on telling him how wonderful I think he is after hearing that story Kelsey told me today.

CHAPTER NINE

onnor

THE DOORBELL INTERRUPTS MY ENJOYMENT OF THE Sunday shows, and I begrudgingly march over to the front door to see who the hell it is. Without looking through the window, I throw the door open to see two of our town's finest in blue standing in front of me.

Great. Just what I need on this fine Sunday morning.

I consider telling them to go away because I want to have a lawyer present for any of their damn questioning, but the idea of spending money to hire one to defend me when I'm innocent rubs me the wrong way. I didn't do anything wrong. What the hell do I need to pay a lawyer for?

We stare each other down for a long moment before I open the storm door and say through gritted teeth, "Gentlemen, what brings you here this morning?"

"Good morning, Mr. Jennings. We'd like to talk to you. Can we come in?" the one I don't like says all smugly, like he knows the choice I have is between talking to them on my front porch and letting them into my house to talk.

Every crime show I've ever seen flashes through my brain as I try to remember if they can simply search a person's house because they've been invited in. No, I don't think they can. Don't they need my permission or a search warrant to do that?

I stop my mind from its frantic spinning by reminding myself that I didn't kill Bryan. I didn't even hurt him. He's to blame for his own death. I'm innocent of whatever they're thinking I did.

So I paste a smile on my face and open the door to let them inside. "I have a few minutes. We can talk in the living room."

The two men hesitate for a split second, just long enough to exchange a glance between them before they walk past me into the house. The girls are still at their sleepover, and Jamie is out in the backyard tending to those ugly flowers she calls her babies, so we should be left alone, at least for a few minutes.

That's all I plan to give them anyway. Whatever they came to tell me has nothing to do with me because I'm innocent.

I offer them a seat on the light gray sofa my wife claimed was the singular piece she absolutely needed that would bring together this room for the sale price of nearly three thousand dollars. I sit in the only chair in the room I enjoy, a far less expensive tan recliner from my first apartment she claims is an eyesore and should be put out for the trash.

Normally, I'd be quite chatty with the police, but something tells me this isn't a visit to let me know they've decided Bryan shot himself and everything's going to be fine for me. I wait silently for them to begin speaking, my stomach twisting into a tight knot with each passing second that I don't hear a word.

Finally, Officer Ramon nods as if any of us has said a thing he could be reacting to and sighs. "Well, Mr. Jennings, we wanted to inform you that the preliminary autopsy shows that your friend, Bryan Corsei, did not commit suicide. He was murdered by a red-blooded, fellow human being."

I shake my head in disbelief, unwilling to believe this nonsense. "That's not true. I saw him wave the gun around and then mistakenly shoot himself. I may not know exactly how it happened or everything about how guns work, but I know when someone shoots themselves. I can discern between suicide and murder, you know."

"The coroner can discern between injuries from suicide and murder too. So we're here to inform you that we're investigating a murder and would like to give you the chance to explain how the angle of the wound says he was shot by someone else and not by his own hand in that clearing on the trails behind the community center."

Both men level their gazes on me, and all I see in their eyes is accusation. I can't believe this. I have no idea how Bryan's wound could say murder to the coroner instead of suicide. I saw him shoot himself, for God's sake!

"But he pointed the gun at his own chest. I witnessed

it with my own eyes. I don't know why the coroner is mistaken, but I know what I saw."

Officer Ramon nods solemnly while his partner Officer Raintree continues to stare daggers at me. "Yes, we have your statement about what happened. That doesn't change the fact that the person trained to know the difference between a gunshot wound that is considered murder and a gunshot wound that's considered suicide has decided it was, indeed, murder. Can you explain how the coroner can be wrong?" Officer Ramon asks with more sincerity than I imagine he's feeling right now.

"Explain how the coroner is wrong? No. I'd suggest if you want to know how he's wrong that you should talk to him. Why are you here giving me a hard time? I saw what I saw. I hurried down to the closest place with a phone to get help. I did everything I should have done as a good citizen. Bryan didn't mean to shoot himself, but that's what happened."

For the first time, Officer Raintree speaks up, and he's as charming as he was yesterday. "But that's not how it happened. There was no suicide. This was a human attacking another human."

"So you think I made up the entire thing about him mistakenly shooting himself? Is that what you came here to tell me?"

Raintree starts to say something, but his partner puts his hand on his arm to stop him. "Mr. Jennings, we simply wanted to give you a chance to clear things up for yourself. That's all we're doing here today," Ramon says.

"Thank you. I think it's time you leave," I say as I stand up and begin walking toward the front door.

They follow me and stop at the door. Raintree glares at me like he's already decided as the judge and jury I'm guilty of Bryan's murder, but Ramon simply sighs deeply and says, "I think you should get yourself a lawyer, Mr. Jennings."

"Thanks for the suggestion, but innocent people don't need attorneys. Goodbye."

I slam the door shut behind them and look down to see my hands shaking like a leaf in a stiff wind. They think I killed my co-worker. I'm the only suspect they're looking at too. I know it.

Good God, how could this have happened? All I wanted to do was get out of the house for a few hours to avoid having to spend time around my wife and eight screaming preteen girls.

WHEN I PULL INTO THE PARKING LOT AT WORK, ALL I can think about is how relieved I am to be here. Even with it being a Monday, I still prefer to be here than at home.

Ever since the terrible events of Saturday, it's like I haven't been able to escape Bryan's death. I can't walk outside into my neighborhood without someone giving me the side eye. The police coming for a visit yesterday didn't help either. At least here, I'll be able to lose myself in my job.

My happiness is quickly dashed the moment I walk into the building. Jerry, the day security guard who has never not greeted anyone without a smile, waves me through the metal detector without so much as a tiny smirk. His pale blue eyes glare at me like I've just told him I killed his dog.

"Mondays, huh?" I say with a smile as I walk past him.

He doesn't answer. In all the years that I've worked here, Jerry has never missed a chance to make small talk. What the hell is wrong with him today?

I know the answer. He heard about Bryan's death, but why does that mean he needs to treat me like some criminal?

"Have a nice day," I mumble as I grab my briefcase off the scanner belt and head down the hallway toward the elevator.

My coworkers Jesse and Carla are waiting, so I stand behind them and hope the elevator arrives soon. I'm not particularly close to either of these people, so it's no surprise they don't speak to me. They seem off today, though. I don't want to be paranoid, but I swear every time they whisper to one another that they're talking about me.

That's crazy. Any other day, I'd stand here just as I am now waiting to ride up in the elevator to the fourth floor and no one would say a word to me, and I'd be perfectly happy. We never chat when we see each other. They work in a different section than I do, and we've never been friendly. Today's no different, yet all I can think as I wait behind them is they're gossiping about me and what happened to Bryan.

The ride up to my floor makes me sure they're talking about me when they continue to whisper to each other and then look back at me like I'm some kind of unwanted thing they wish they could dispel from this elevator. I consider asking what the problem is, but the last thing I want to hear this morning is how they think I'm a goddamned murderer.

By the time I reach my desk, I'm positive I was mistaken about work being some kind of refuge for me. It's just as bad as staying at home and dealing with the ugly judgmental stares from my neighbors. Great. I just hope none of my leads have heard what happened, or I'm going to have a hard time selling a damn thing.

Mid-morning break time comes around, but unlike every other workday, nobody asks me if I'm going to grab a coffee or try one of Sylvia's cakes she makes for everyone every Monday. The entire office empties out until I'm left alone at my desk, thankful that it seems I'm only a leper in my community and workplace and not around the world where my clients are.

At least there's that.

Out of the corner of my eye, I see Martin standing in his office doorway. He waves me over as he tries to smile, but it never reaches his eyes. Great. I'm probably going to be fired now. He'll probably spew that shtick about moral turpitude like he did when he fired Meredith for having an affair with the maintenance guy. If he's willing to let someone go for sleeping around, I can't imagine being safe in my job now that he thinks I'm a damn murderer.

Every step I take toward him feels like a move toward doom. Without this job, I can't afford the mortgage. Or the girls' gymnastic lessons and everything that comes with their competitions. Or the landscaper who comes once a week to make sure the lawn is cut to the proper specifications that goddamned HOA insists are necessary to keep our community looking the best it can be.

God, I hate when one of the board says those words. They always come attached to a tone that's full of irritation mixed with condescension. Every single one of those people who lord the rules over us acts as if the Almighty himself placed them in their position of power. What a bunch of assholes!

All of this fills my head as I walk past my boss into his office. He closes the door behind us, which is never a good sign. Martin always kept the door open when he and Bryan would hang out in here. That's how we all knew he was the favorite.

"I thought I should bring you in so we could have a talk this morning, Connor. How are you doing?"

Surprise stops me from answering for a few moments. How am I doing? Nobody's asked me that since everything happened on Saturday. Not even Jamie has shown any concern for how I'm feeling.

He sits down behind his desk and smiles for the first time. "You look tired. This whole thing has taken a toll on you, I bet."

I nod, unsure how to answer. If I complain about how I'm being treated, I'll sound like a Grade A asshole considering Bryan's dead. If I pretend like I'm fine, I'll come off as cold and uncaring, like his horrible death hasn't bothered me at all.

Martin leans forward and nods solemnly. "For what it's worth, I don't think you did anything to hurt Bryan. It's not in your nature, Connor. It's just not."

My surprise morphs into genuine shock. "Really?

Because everyone else thinks I killed him," I say in a low voice, barely able to utter those horrible words.

"I know, and I'm sorry for the way they're treating you."

I let out a heavy sigh, finally able to feel some relief from how awful all this has been. "I get it. It's a small town we all live in. They see the cops come to my house, so they assume the worst. I had hoped my coworkers would know me better than that, but at least you don't think the worst of me. I appreciate that, Martin."

He doesn't respond, and for a few very long moments, we sit there in silence. A feeling of awkwardness settles in between us in the quiet, and I can't help but worry at any moment Martin is going to say as much as he hates to do this, he can't have someone like me working for the company with all the discontent my being here is causing. I couldn't blame him if he did.

But instead, he sighs and asks, "What happened? Can you tell me? I'm hearing all sorts of ridiculous and outrageous stories I can't imagine are anything but ridiculous gossip."

As much as I hate recounting every step of that horrible afternoon, I feel like I need to for the only person in the world I have supporting me. I take a deep breath in and let it out slowly as the memory of everything that happened fills my brain once more.

"Bryan and I decided to go for a hike. My kids had some of their friends over, and the last thing I wanted to do was listen to eight screaming and giggling girls for another minute longer. So I met him at the community center, and we set off on the trail right behind the building. We weren't out there for long before we came to the clearing at the top of the first hill."

Martin nods. "I know exactly the place. Bryan convinced me to get off my duff one Sunday morning and go hiking with him, and we walked up to that same clearing. I was out of breath because I'm not in the kind of shape he is."

Suddenly my boss stops and frowns, drawing his eyebrows in toward his nose in a deep grimace. "Was. I have to tell you I'm not sure I'm ever going to get used to talking about him in the past tense."

I feel like I want to say I'm sorry, but I know that will sound like I'm guilty, so I simply force a tiny smile and nod. Martin closes his eyes, and I watch as he fights back tears. He and Bryan really must have been close.

When his grief subsides, he opens his eyes and says, "So what happened?"

"I don't know, Martin. He was waving a gun around, chasing after some hedgehog he saw in the bushes. It wasn't doing anything. He just seemed to want to kill it. He took a shot at it, and it ran away. He wanted to take another shot, but I said we should keep hiking. I don't know what he was thinking, but he waved the gun around again and I heard it go off. The next thing I knew, he was on the ground with a shot to his chest. I didn't have my phone, so I ran down to the community center. But the police are telling me they think I shot him, that it has to be a murder and not a suicide. I swear on my life I wouldn't hurt Bryan. I liked him. He was a good guy. Why would I want to do anything to him?"

He nods while I try to explain everything and hope I

don't sound like a complete moron. It was suicide, not murder. I'd stake my life on that.

"The difference in the angle of the gunshot should be telling them it was self-inflicted," my boss says.

I shrug, wishing I knew why they can't see that. "I don't know why this has blown up into a huge case. It was an accident. I don't think Bryan meant to hurt himself or me, for that matter. I think he believed he could handle a gun, and like it can, it went off when he didn't expect it to. I swear I wouldn't kill a soul, Martin."

"There's no way you killed him. I don't believe that, and I never will. You don't have it in you to be a killer, Connor. I'd stake my entire life savings on that fact."

"Well, I wish you were in charge of the investigation then because the cops are sure it's me. They told me I need to get a lawyer. I can't afford that. Between my house, my cars, and my kids' extracurriculars, I barely have enough to put food on the table. Jamie keeps telling me that it's all going to pay off when the girls get into a college they want on a free ride for gymnastics, and all I can say is I hope to God that happens because if I have to pay for both of them to go to school after how much it cost to keep them in all the activities they've required all these years, I don't know what I'm going to do."

My words begin to sound frantic as I explain how downright poor I am, and even though I should be embarrassed, I'm not. Being the only one who works in my family has become an albatross around my neck. I'm not ashamed to admit it or that I can't pay for a lawyer, even if I need one.

Martin tries to calm me down with some kind words, but the reality is that's my life. I make good money, and it goes out as fast as it comes in. Trying to explain that to my wife and kids is like talking to a brick wall. They only see the things they need and want. The truth that money only goes so far isn't of any interest to them.

"Take it easy. It's all going to be okay. You're going to be fine. The police are going to pull their heads out of their asses and figure out the truth of what happened to Bryan. Just take a deep breath. Try to keep some perspective. I know it's hard, but you're going to be okay. You have a lovely wife and two beautiful girls. Just focus on taking care of them. As for work and the people here, I'm going to have a conversation with the two or three I think are the ringleaders causing you trouble. You shouldn't have to dread coming to work. No innocent man should. We're a family here. It's time your coworkers remember that."

What I dread is the idea of my boss getting involved at all. Shaking my head, I say, "No, Martin. Please don't. That will only make things worse. People are going to believe what they believe. We can't change that. I had hoped they'd know better because they know the kind of person I am, but they're free to think what they want. I know I'm innocent, and I'm glad you think I am too. That's enough for now."

My boss's expression fills with concern. "Are you sure? I don't want to see you become some office punching bag. It's not right, and it makes my job harder, to be honest. I'd like to say something to make sure they remember to act professionally. No one is saying they need to throw you a party, but at the very least, I think they need to be reminded that no matter what happens, civility is the name of the game at this company."

I can see there's no way I'm going to talk him out of having some big group meeting with the people in this office, so I merely smile and pray to God it won't turn into some terrible thing that causes even more resentment toward me. I can't afford to lose this job. I just can't.

"Okay. Thanks, Martin. Break time is almost over, so I think I'm going to go back to my desk and see if I can get some work done. Our products don't sell themselves, right?"

I punctuate my question with a smile that nearly kills me, but I force it anyway. He's the only person in my corner right now, so I need to keep him happy.

As I stand to leave, he joins me and walks me to the door. Patting me on the shoulder, he says, "You're a good person, Connor. I know this is going to work out for the best. The truth will prevail. Don't worry. Karma always does her job."

I head back to my desk with that last sentence of his ringing in my ears. *Karma always does her job.* Is that really true?

And if so, is that what's happening to me now?

CHAPTER TEN

amie

CASSANDRA AND DANIELLE WHISPER BETWEEN themselves in the back seat, and I smile as I remember being a young teenage girl with a crush on some boy. I'm glad my girls have one another. I didn't have a sister, but I did have a friend named Julie back then. We told each another everything, especially when it came to boys. Neither one of us were allowed to date until we turned sixteen, but I can't count the number of nights she slept over at my house or I slept over at hers and we stayed up all night gossiping about all the boys we liked.

My daughters aren't anywhere close to the age when they'll be able to date, but I've caught them talking about some boy in Cassandra's class one of them likes. Connor and I have never spoken about it, but I think maybe we should let the girls date earlier than my parents let me. I'm not as worried about everything like my mother was, and I definitely trust the girls more than my parents trusted me.

Maybe it's time to talk to my husband about them dating.

I look up at the rearview mirror and see they look upset. Oh, I remember that too. The tears and recriminations over some boy who didn't feel the same way as I did. There's no pain for a young girl like unrequited love. My mother never wanted to talk about that with me, but I'm a different kind of mom.

"Everything okay with you two?" I ask as casually as I can while I continue to drive them to practice.

I glance up at the rearview mirror again, and this time I see tears in Danielle's eyes. She's always been the more sensitive of my girls, so I'm not surprised.

"What's wrong, honey?" I ask as Cassandra angrily grumbles something.

My younger child simply shakes her head before looking down at her legs, so my older child speaks up. "Mom, somebody said something to Danielle and me in school. It wasn't nice."

Much tougher, even as a younger child, Cassandra can always be relied on to defend her sister. I'm glad she's that way. She sees injustice in the world and never fails to speak up. I hope she knows how proud I am of her for that.

"I bet you told them isn't wasn't nice, didn't you?" I ask her with a smile.

But neither of my daughters are smiling back at me.

Cassandra leans forward so she can poke her head

between the two front seats. "Mom, it was bad. Danielle spent her whole lunch hiding out in the bathroom."

I turn my head and see her expression is deadly serious. What in the world could have happened at school today?

Thankfully, my girls are usually happy to tell me all about their days, so I absolutely feel I can ask. "Well, what did this person say to upset your sister so much?"

In a low voice, Cassandra says, "They said that Daddy killed someone, and he's a murderer."

Fear tears through me, making my blood practically run cold. The whispers have already begun. I thought I had made sure to put a stop to them before they started by talking to Vanessa. So much for that being the fix.

Steadying my voice, I force a smile and say, "Oh, kids can say the wildest things. It's usually because they heard something at home from their parents. I'm sure it's all a mistake, honey."

That seems to make Cassandra happy, but when I look into the back seat, I see Danielle with her head in her hands. "Oh, honey, don't cry. I know kids can be cruel, but it's fine. Your father couldn't hurt a fly. Don't pay attention to gossip."

My younger daughter drops her hands from her face and wipes the tears under her eyes. "Marissa was so mean when she said that Daddy's a murderer. I didn't want to cry, but she made me so angry."

Like me, Danielle gets very emotional when she gets upset. Cassandra can control herself, but as has happened so many times in my life, when her younger sister gets angry, she can't hold back the tears. She hates it as much as I hate that it happens to me, but neither of us seem to know how to control our emotions.

"It's okay, baby. People say a lot of things. That doesn't mean we have to care about each and every one of them. Let it go and focus on your practice today. That'll make you feel better."

Cassandra picks up on what I'm trying to do and sits back with her sister. "Yeah, Mom's right. Forget that idiot Marissa. She's always so mean. Do you remember when you got the best grade in English class, and she started that rumor that you cheated? Nobody believed that because they knew you were the smartest kid in your class. Forget her. We have bigger things to do today. Remember you said you wanted to work on that double flip? We can do that after coach says we have free time, okay?"

"Okay," Danielle says with a sniffle. "That sounds good."

I love how my girls take care of one another. I also love that they know they can tell me anything, especially the upsetting things. They may not be very close to Connor since he's never been a big fan of being a girl dad, but at least they know they have me solidly in their corner at all times.

"There you go. I'm so proud of you two. I hope you know that. You're strong and smart and you watch out for one another."

Neither of them say anything to that, but when I look up at the rearview mirror to see what they're doing, Danielle has a smile on her face while Cassandra looks like she could take on the world. Good. I hope they forget what that Marissa said.

I pull up to the front of the building where practice will be held and consider going in to watch, but now that both girls have made the team, I don't need to do that. Instead, I'll just pop over to the café and enjoy a coffee while I wait.

"Okay, you two. Have a wonderful practice! I'll be here to pick you up when you're done."

My daughters get out of the car and wave goodbye to me before I put the car in gear to leave. I wave to Vanessa, but she doesn't wave back. She looks like she may not have seen me.

I'm sure I'll see her when I come back to get the girls. For now, I need a coffee.

The parking lot of the café is practically empty when I arrive, but I'm not unhappy since that means I'll get my choice of where to sit. I had hoped to talk to Kelsey again and possibly hear more about that story she told me the other day. She's so different from everyone else I know around here that I can't help but want to know more about her life.

It takes me no time at all to get my iced latte and heated scone with butter, a trick I will forever be grateful to Kelsey for now that I never have to endure another bone-dry scone again. Since there's only one other person in the coffee shop—an older man I'm guessing must be at least sixty by the headful of steel gray hair—I'm able to grab a seat near the window at the back of the restaurant. It's quiet, just like I want on a Monday.

Unfortunately, I don't get to enjoy the silence for long. A group of women come in, noisy and uncertain about what they want as they stand up at the counter. Then Maris walks in like she's a woman on a mission.

What is she doing here? She should be watching her daughter's practice. Poor Tiffanie is never going to be put on the team if her mother isn't there.

Maris spots me immediately and rushes back to where I'm sitting. Red in the face and flushed, she looks like she's just run all the way here from practice. She stops beside me to catch her breath, hanging on to the edge of the table like she may collapse at any moment.

"Are you okay?" I ask, suddenly concerned something may be genuinely wrong. "Sit down. You look exhausted, Maris."

She tries to say some words, but they all get swallowed up by her huffing and puffing. So instead of trying to prod her along to tell me what's going on, I simply wait, sipping my iced latte.

When Maris finally catches her breath, she takes my suggestion and sits down across from me. Now calm, her eyes are filled with what looks like utter panic.

Damn. She probably just found out Tiffanie isn't going to be making the team this year. I need to be sure to act surprised, although I don't think a single person at those practices would be shocked the poor kid didn't do well enough.

Maris takes one last big breath before she finally begins to speak. "Jamie, I rushed over here as soon as I heard what everyone was saying. I tried your house first, but when you weren't there, I remembered you saying you liked to relax here while your girls are practicing. I'm so sorry. How are you holding up, you poor thing?"

Those last words hit me like a slap to the face. You poor thing? Am I some wretched creature who deserves pity? Why is she acting like I am?

I smile, sure she's mistaken about whatever tragedy she's talking about. "I'm fine, Maris. Relax. Whatever you heard, it's not real."

The stress visibly drains from her body, and she leans back against the chair, smiling. "Oh, thank God! I hated hearing what everyone was saying. I didn't think it was true."

Now I'm curious, so I ask, "What did you hear? I hope it was something like I'm having a wild life I'm trying to keep a secret. I get the feeling I've become downright boring lately."

Her smile fades away before she shakes her head as the look of worry returns. "Jamie, you don't know?"

Maris isn't the brightest bulb in the box, so I laugh and answer, "No, obviously not. I just hope it's juicy gossip about me. You know what they say. There's no such thing as bad publicity."

"Well, this is bad, but it's not really about you. Everyone at practice was talking about how Connor…"

She stops and leans over the table so our faces are barely six inches apart. Whispering so I can barely hear her, she continues. "They're saying he shot someone, Jamie. That Connor is the person who killed that poor man up on the nature paths. I heard Kayleigh's mother say she overheard a couple of the cops talking at that vegan restaurant that just opened up, and they supposedly said they're going to arrest him!"

I listen to all she has to say, horrified that this little problem of Connor's has now become all anyone can talk about in town. After all I've done to ensure our daughters have the best chance at success, he has to go and screw it up.

Damn him!

Even though I'm angry at my husband, I can't show Maris that. I can't even show her this new gossip about him, and by extension about me and the girls, bothers me.

So I force a smile I need to look genuine and wave my hand as if to make it seem like none of what she's told me bothers me in the least. "Oh, it's all a mistake. Connor is devastated by the man's death, but he had no part in it. The man accidently shot himself. It's unfortunate, but it's no one's fault. I do appreciate you worrying about me, though. Thank you, Maris."

She has no idea how much effort it took to say all of that. I want to scream and run out of this coffee shop in humiliation. I've worked assiduously day in and day out to make sure my family is never part of the sordid gossip that permeates the gymnastics practices, and now because of Connor and some jackass who doesn't know how to handle a gun, all four of us are being talked about at this very moment.

Maris reaches across the table and gives my hand a sympathetic squeeze. "I'm so happy to hear this! You know how the mothers at gymnastics can be. I didn't think any of it was true, but I knew I had to make sure you knew about what they're saying."

Once more, I wave away her concern even as mine grows by leaps and bounds. "No, it's all good. Our community is a very small one, so I'm not surprised to hear someone's running with this tale. I mean, a man did die, so I wish they'd be a bit more sensitive to that, but it's nothing new. The mothers will gossip about anything."

Then a horrible thought fills my brain. Have my girls heard this terrible rumor at practice? That's supposed to be a safe place for them. How dare those mothers do this to them!

I don't want Maris to think I'm giving any credence to what's being said, but I have to know if the girls are being spared the gossip. It's bad enough that girl at school said something to Danielle. I don't want their place on the gymnastics squad to be in danger because of this rumor.

"My girls didn't hear any of this, did they? I'd hate for them to hear grown women saying something cruel about their father."

Quickly, Maris shakes her head. "No, I don't think so. It was mostly just the talk up in the stands. You know, where we all sit while the girls practice? I don't think they could hear anything they were talking about, thankfully."

I smile and nod like everything's okay, but I can't help but wonder why Vanessa didn't handle this after our conversation last night. She clearly knows that rumor isn't true since we spoke about that very topic, so why isn't she stopping it?

So much for nipping things in the bud.

As much as I want to run out of this café right now, I know I can't. Appearance is everything, and if Maris thinks I'm even a tiny bit bothered by what she told me, she'll assume there's a kernel of truth to it.

I lean back in my chair and crack my neck, smiling the entire time. "You know what I think I need to get back to? Yoga. I haven't been to a class in over a month, and I'm starting to really feel it."

For a few moments, she seems confused, but then she nods her head and returns the smile. "I'm the same way. If I let any time pass, I'm as stiff as a board. Can you believe that? I'm not even thirty, and I'm already feeling like a sixty-year-old woman."

The two of us laugh at that, but for me, it's all an act. My world is crashing down around me, and I have no choice but to sit here and smile as if nothing is wrong.

I've seen what can happen when a rumor like this isn't quashed quickly. A woman named Jenna a few years ago became the subject of horrible gossip saying she was cheating on her husband, whose name I can't remember anymore. Her daughter Katlyn was a new girl at gymnastics, and she had real talent that could have helped the team.

None of that mattered once those mothers got wind of the rumor about Jenna. It didn't matter that it was entirely untrue. The man some of the women had seen her with was her brother, and everything was easily explained away.

Still, they talked about her so much that she never wanted to stay to watch the girls practice, and once she was gone, her daughter never had a chance. The mothers pressured the coach to leave Katlyn off the team, even though it hurt the squad, and before long, the girl dropped out. The last I heard, the family had moved away, disgusted by how ugly their neighbors had made things for them, and all over a misunderstanding none of the mothers would admit.

I need to figure out how to fix this mess before it ruins everything for my family.

CHAPTER ELEVEN

onnor

ALONE AT THE DINNER TABLE, I ENJOY A MOMENT OF peace before my wife and daughters join me. The smell of some kind of roast fills the air as Jamie scurries around the kitchen getting things ready. She mumbles something about asparagus being better with extra virgin olive oil, but I don't bother to ask what she means. My wife routinely talks to herself about things I don't give a damn about. I'm not even sure she cares about the things she says. I think it's just her way of filling the silence, which she seems to hate.

For me, silence is a luxury I don't get to experience enough. If I could have a week of pure peace and quiet, I'd think I died and went to heaven. Not having to listen to anything about work or my wife's complaints about needing something or the girls' requests for more and more things they absolutely, positively must have would be a dream come true.

Unfortunately, that's all it's ever going to be. A dream.

"Connor, did you pick up the mail on your way in from getting home from work?" my wife calls from the kitchen.

I'm literally ten feet away from where she's standing. Why she needs to yell is beyond me. And why can't she just ask when she sits down with me to eat at the same table?

I don't answer her question and simply walk to the front door to check for the mail. The woman is home all day. Why can't she get the mail?

The answer to that question remains a mystery, and I get a few envelopes out of the mailbox. Bills. Something from our cell phone carrier about the newest iPhone. One addressed to me in someone's handwriting. You don't see too many of those anymore. Probably from that politician who claims voting for him is like casting a vote for your best friend. He always uses that handwritten letter gimmick.

I toss the stack of mail onto the hallway table and head back to the dining room. By the time I get there, my daughters are already in their seats and complaining about something.

Just one week of peace and quiet is all I ask. Maybe a week is too much to expect. How about a day? Or simply an hour?

"Dad, you have to make those cops stop coming to our house," my daughter Danielle whines as her sister nods her head in agreement.

"Trust me, honey. I want them to stay away as much as you do."

"But you have to do it right now!" she continues. "Nobody at school will talk to us because everyone says you're a murderer."

Now I get to hear this nonsense from my own flesh and blood. Great.

"I'm sure it will be fine, girls. Just wait. A day or two and this will all blow over."

What I really want to say is get the hell off my back, but letting my temper get the best of me right now isn't going to make things any better. It would be nice if my wife would be on my side this one time, but I'm not expecting miracles.

"But Dad! None of the girls at practice wanted to be around us today," Cassandra squeals, following up on her sister's complaints, as if I didn't understand the first time I heard them.

My wife sets the green and yellow platter with slices of roast pork in the center of the table, and for a brief moment, the delicious scent of the garlic and rosemary she used floats into my nostrils, and I forget how shitty my life is. A second later, though, my daughters' whining and their mother's concern that their entire lives are going to be ruined because no one wants to be friends with them fill my ears.

"Connor, two of the mothers declined my invitation to have their daughters over next weekend. They were very cold and distant when they did too. And Vanessa Dennis didn't wave back when I waved to her outside the gym. I'm worried we'll have to move if this keeps up."

Before I can stop myself, I stab my fork into a slice of pork and drop it on my plate as I say, "Move? Nobody's moving. We're upside down on this house right now. Moving would only make our money problems worse, so I don't want to hear another damn word about moving."

"I don't want to move!" Danielle screams. Folding her arms across her chest, she adds, "I won't move. I won't!"

That's it. I've had enough of these people. I'm home for not a whole hour, and the entire time not a single damn one of them has even thought to ask how I'm doing with all this. I was with someone who died in front of me. Everyone's accusing me of killing him, and all my family can think of is themselves.

"Enough!" I bark and then stand up to leave. "I can't listen to you three anymore. We're not moving, so that's that. I don't care if people won't talk to you. I'm being accused of a heinous crime, and all you three can talk about is how it affects you."

The three of them stare up at me with utter judgment in their eyes like I'm the villain in this little play they're producing. Nope. Not today. I will not let these people make things worse for me with all that I'm dealing with since Bryan's death. Not going to happen. I'm done.

I storm away as my wife calls after me, "Connor, where are you going?"

Like she gives a damn. She's probably worried I might march right over to that ridiculous gymnastics school and tell them I won't be paying another dime to their little clique. Then what social life would she have? Let's see how she likes losing the respect of people she cares about.

"Out! I'll be back later," I snap on my way out the front door.

The fresh air instantly makes me feel better, but truthfully, it wouldn't matter if I walked out into a downpour of hail. I don't want to go back to that house. How sad is that? I pay for that house. Every day I go to work to ensure that house stays ours, and now I can't stand the idea of returning to it.

The sun sits just above the horizon, sending out gorgeous shades of purple and orange as it readies itself to set. It's a beautiful sight, one that I rarely get to enjoy, and I stop at the end of my street to really look at it.

After a minute or so, I sense eyes on me, and I look around to see neighbors—my neighbors who I've lived around for over a decade—standing on their lawns speaking in hushed voices and then turning to stare at me. These are people I've lent tools to and attended cookouts at their houses in the summer. They're people who've been to my house for cocktails and who send their kids to my front door every time they have something to sell.

Yet now, I'm not good enough to even receive a friendly wave, much less a kind hello. No, I'm simply a pariah they think is nothing more than someone to gossip about and shun, sure I've done the worst thing they can imagine.

So much for that wonderful sense of community those HOA assholes are always preaching.

I hurry away, eager to not feel like some kind of wretched criminal with all eyes on him. I've lived in this neighborhood for eleven years. These people know me. How could they think I'd kill Bryan?

Judgmental bastards. And here I thought they were my friends.

My feet seem to have a mind of their own, and I end up on the very path Bryan and I walked two days ago. I'm alone as I walk into that clearing where everything took place. All I can think about is how the police said his injuries show he was murdered and didn't commit suicide.

That's impossible. I saw what happened with my own eyes. He was waving the goddamned gun around and accidentally shot himself. How the hell is the damn coroner getting that wrong?

Was there another person in that clearing with the two of us? That's the only way this murder idea makes any sense. But if we weren't alone, wouldn't I have seen them?

No! That's bullshit. Bryan screwed up and mistakenly pointed the gun at himself. There couldn't have been a person with us in that clearing. I'd remember that.

Jesus, I'm starting to think maybe I'm mistaken. Maybe there was someone there in addition to Bryan and me? Did that person shoot him? Wouldn't I have heard another gunshot?

None of this makes sense.

Turning three hundred and sixty degrees, I try to find some evidence that whoever may have shot Bryan was here, but I'm not even sure what to look for. I'd think the cops would have found something, but since they're so laser-focused on me, I guess it's not surprising they haven't.

Those two aren't exactly talented at their jobs. Who knew our local police were so incompetent?

As I question whether or not I'm beginning to go insane, out of the corner of my eye I see someone in the brush down the path from the clearing. I immediately make a beeline to where they stand, but in a flash, there's no one there.

I am losing my mind.

No. I saw what I saw. The other day and now. Whatever this is, whether it be shadows because it's twilight or something else, I know what I saw.

"Come out and show yourself! I know you're here."

I wait for whoever it was a moment ago to answer or come out into the open, but nothing happens. Maybe I am seeing things. If not, how can I explain thinking there was a person in front of me no more than ten feet away one moment and them disappearing the next?

The sound of someone stepping on a branch behind me makes me spin around, and what I see makes my heart skip a beat. It can't be. No, that's not possible. Now I know my mind is playing tricks on me because that person can't be here.

I open my mouth to speak to what I'm sure is a ghost, but before I can say a word, something hard slams into the back of my head. My knees buckle, and then I collapse to the ground with the last image I see being impossible.

SOMETHING PRESSING ON MY SHOULDER WAKES ME UP, and I open my eyes to see Officer Ramon standing over me shining a flashlight in my face. A throbbing pain at the back of my head reminds me that I didn't merely fall asleep here on the pathway.

Someone knocked me out.

Then I remember who I saw right before everything went black. But I must have been wrong. I couldn't have seen her.

She's dead.

Was it all a dream? My mind must be playing tricks on me. That's the only explanation for what's going on.

"Mr. Jennings, what are you doing here? It's the middle of the night, for God's sake."

I scrub the sleep from my eyes and slowly sit up as I try to formulate an answer that doesn't sound like I'm out of my mind. Confused by what he said about it being the middle of the night, I look around and see it's pitch black out, except for his flashlight aimed at the ground next to me.

"What time is it?"

"Nearly one o'clock in the morning. Now what are you doing here?"

One o'clock. I must have been out for nearly six hours.

"I was taking a walk and came up here to try to figure out what happened the other day," I say as the events of my night slowly come back to me.

Pointing his flashlight directly into my eyes, he asks, "So you came up here and just decided to take a nap right here on the ground?"

The way he says that, like he's dealing with a madman or an idiot, and that fucking light practically burning out my retinas make me want to strangle him. I contain my anger, though, and shield my eyes as I stand up.

"No. Someone attacked me from behind. They hit me with something heavy, and I collapsed. I must have been passed out here the whole time."

I gently run my fingertips over the back of my head and feel a hard lump bigger than a golf ball. Jesus, what the hell did they use to hit me?

"Someone attacked you? Why would they do that?" Officer Ramon asks in a tone that tells me he doesn't believe a word I'm saying.

Exasperated by this man's inability to see a crime when it's occurred, I point to the back of my head and snap, "Run your fingers over my scalp, and you'll feel where they hit me. Maybe if you people weren't so busy condemning me as judge and jury you'd be able to see this isn't a case of me killing someone. And now, you've gotten people around here so worked up that they're coming after me, Officer Ramon."

He looks at me like he doesn't believe a word I say but then does as I suggested and runs his hand over the back of my head where they hit me. It hurts like nothing I've ever experienced, but I try not to yell out as his fat hand clumsily touches the sensitive area.

"See? I'm not lying. I didn't just fall asleep up here. I was knocked out. Who did it I have no idea."

That makes him smirk. "So you didn't shoot your friend, but someone now has it out for you?"

This guy is a total tool. How did my community hire this guy to be a cop? Were there no better applicants? Probably that shitty group of HOA assholes. No doubt they loved him the moment he came in for the interview. Like saw like and they fell in love.

"I still stand by my statement that Bryan accidentally shot himself. For God's sake, how does that coroner not know that the angle of the wound is different between when someone shoots a man and when he shoots himself? Jesus, what does it take for you guys to see that I'm not the person who killed Bryan?"

Officer Ramon doesn't answer any of my questions, so I continue. "And as for why someone would have it out for me, what did you think would happen when you and your buddy visited my house? You've repeatedly treated me like a criminal, and now everyone else is following suit. Maybe you should have tried a little professionalism and not used the court of public opinion to convict me. Is that how you two usually conduct yourselves?"

His eyebrows shoot up into his forehead at my question. It seems I've offended my community's finest. Too bad. Maybe now they'll try to do some investigating instead of fixating on me.

But then he speaks again, and I know I'm getting nowhere with him.

"All I see is a man who's hit his head. Nothing else. You're going to have to come down to the station, Mr. Jennings."

I wish I could tell them all I saw and not just about my unseen attacker. The problem is the person I saw with my own eyes right before something hit my head can't be here. It just isn't possible.

As Officer Ramon begins to guide me back down the path toward the community center, I try to piece together what's going on. Am I being set up? I must be. But that doesn't explain me seeing someone who's been dead for over fifteen years.

Together, we ride to the police station as I try to figure out just what the hell is going on. Why am I seeing someone who can't possibly be anywhere but six feet in the ground?

This is madness. I'm losing my mind. Even worse, this officer doesn't believe a word I say.

Is this karma come to give me my just desserts?

By the time I sit down in the police station interrogation room, I'm convinced that's exactly what's happening. It's the only way any of this makes sense. Karma has come to finally make me pay for what I did all those years ago.

We sit down in a small room that reminds me of the school I attended as an elementary student. Just like at Roosevelt School, the walls are painted a dark beige on the upper half of the wall and a deep brown on the bottom half. It's an ugly, institutional look that suits my companions perfectly.

Officers Ramon and Raintree face me from the other side of the black metal table with a leg that's too short, so every time anyone leans on the top of it, the table wobbles. You'd think they'd fold up a piece of paper or something to level things off. Real problem solvers these two are.

I watch as Raintree, who I secretly call Surly Raintree, plants his elbow in front of him and three pens roll away toward the floor. Ramon reaches over him to catch them and sets them near him. It's like these two are comedy clowns. They just don't know it.

"So, Mr. Jennings, you say you were up on the trail trying to figure out who killed Bryan Corsei," Surly Raintree says with a sneer.

For the umpteenth time, I answer, "Yes."

That gets me a squint and a long glare before he continues. "Well, that's interesting because a witness has come forward to say she saw you kill Mr. Corsei."

His claim stuns me for a moment, but I quickly regroup and ask, "Who?"

Suddenly, both officers don't seem to have a thing to say. They merely shake their heads, as if I asked them if either would like a soda.

"Who? Who said that? I want to know because they're lying."

Officer Ramon shakes his head again. "I'm sorry, but we can't divulge that information yet. This is still an active investigation."

I'm beginning to get frustrated with the two-thirds of the Three Stooges I have to deal with here. What I want to do is lash out, but I know these geniuses will think that's some kind of evidence of my guilt, so I take a deep breath and blow it out of my mouth in a rush to calm myself down.

"As much as I can't understand why I need to say this again, here goes. I ran down to the community center to get help. Let me ask you this. Did the girl there see any blood on me? Any at all? No. Did you when you arrived on the scene? No. You say I shot Bryan in the chest. Don't you think I'd have some blood on me if I did that? Now I'm no expert in that kind of injury, but I'd think with all the arteries in that part of the body there'd be a lot of blood loss. Wouldn't the killer get at least a little on them? Really, guys. I know you've gotten yourselves fixed on me, but I didn't do it."

Neither one of them seems to either understand what I'm saying or care. They don't say a word to refute my logic. They simply sit there staring at me.

Disgusted that once again they won't listen, I stand up and ask, "Are you arresting me?"

Raintree looks like he just swallowed something gross and wants to throw up, but Ramon merely shakes his head and answers with a quiet, "No."

"Then I'm leaving. Thanks for being so helpful to a person left for dead on a secluded trail. You're doing a hellava job here, guys."

So much for thinking the police are going to figure this out. Clearly, they've decided it's me, and they don't believe they need to look for anyone else.

I want to say this will all turn out fine because I'm innocent, but I know the truth isn't that easy.

CHAPTER TWELVE

amie

MY MIND SPINS AS I TRY TO FIGURE OUT WHAT TO DO. All my best laid plans lie in smithereens. My daughters and I have become modern day lepers. All of this because of Connor, the one who's never done a damn thing to help Cassandra and Danielle other than pay for their gymnastics lessons. I'm the one who's schmoozed the coach and the other mothers so our girls can be sure to succeed.

Nobody understands what I've had to do. Was Connor the one who sat there listening to those horrible women trash people and had to paste a smile on his face when the whole time he wanted to stand up and scream, "You women are awful bitches! Why does anyone talk to you?"

No, it was me. Was it him who worked all the bake sales, car washes, and every other event that came down the line from school and gymnastics? Of course not. He has a real job, as he likes to remind me. He works all day so we can have everything we want. He practically hangs himself on the cross for that every time I bring up helping with anything.

Well, who told me to not work when the girls went to school full-time? I wanted to get a job so we could afford to go on vacations and do all the things we want to do without pinching pennies. It was Connor who shot down my idea, even when I suggested I could get a part-time position somewhere. He claimed it was because of all the times the girls have off from school during the year since neither of us would have wanted to leave them home alone, but I got the sense that it was more about his ego than anything else.

What would the world think when they saw his wife working? That kind of thinking is ridiculous nowadays. It's not the fifties, for God's sake. Women work outside the home now, and if I had gotten a job when I wanted to, our lives would have been so much easier by now. We'd be able to travel and buy whatever we wanted if both of us worked, but because he decided I shouldn't work, the girls and I have to listen to him complain almost daily about how much the things we want cost.

All of this marches through my mind as I drive to the coffee shop after dropping the girls off at school this morning. I hated seeing the look of dread in both their beautiful faces when I stopped to let them out of the car. They shouldn't fear anything at their age. I pretended like everything is going to be fine, but I don't know if that's true.

By the time I pull into the parking lot, I can't deny I'm filled with dread too. What if one of the mothers from gymnastics is there? I don't think I can handle any more snubbing.

God, how did my life turn into this?

With every step I take toward the coffee shop front door, all I can think of is how much I'd like to see someone who thinks this entire mess of Connor's is all a mistake. Why are people so damn quick to jump to conclusions? Our neighbors and friends have already decided he's guilty, despite the fact that they've known us for years and know he couldn't hurt a fly.

What a mess.

I take a deep breath to steady my nerves and fling open the glass door before walking in, immediately scanning the café for anyone I know. How awful is that? I'm actively hoping not to see people I've known for years.

The server walks up to the register as I take my position in front of the counter to order, and I nervously scan her expression to see if she's hating me today too. She doesn't seem upset to see me. To test that, I give her a tiny smile, and she immediately returns it.

Relief washes over me that at least one person today doesn't appear to be unhappy I'm around. I've never really paid much attention to this young woman, but now that she seems to be the sole person who doesn't hate me, I notice how pretty her blue eyes are. They remind me of that light shade of blue my bridesmaids wore.

After ordering my iced latte and heated cranberry-orange scone with butter, I smile again and say, "Thank you. By the way, your eyes are a beautiful shade of blue."

For a second, I worry I overstepped my bounds because she stares at me without saying a word, but then finally, she flashes me a big smile. "Thank you! That's so sweet of you to say. They used to be darker blue, but my grandmother told me that blue eyes fade as we get older. At this rate, my eyes will be the palest blue possible by the time I reach her age!"

We share a laugh, and for a few moments, I don't dread my life. This person I've never paid much attention to before today will probably never know it, but her kindness is exactly what I needed this morning.

"Give me a minute or two, and I'll have your order up for you," she says before spinning on her heel and heading over to where she makes customers' coffees.

Just as I'm relaxing, I hear the door open and instinctively look over to see if I know who's coming into the café. Not a second later, dread fills me again, but only for a moment until I realize I don't recognize the woman walking in with a baby in a stroller.

This emotional rollercoaster is going to make me sick. I don't understand why people are treating my family and me like this. Even if Connor did do something to that man, and I have a difficult time believing that, what does it have to do with me and the girls?

When the young barista serves me my items, I smile again and walk to a table back in the corner where hopefully no one will notice me. Lost in my own misery about all that's happened, I don't see Kelsey until she clears her throat.

Looking up, I smile at her, noticing she's wearing a

really cute sundress, and instantly hope she hasn't heard the terrible rumors. "Hey, how are you today?"

She always looks very serious, so I hope her expression now isn't an indication that she's heard what happened up on that trail and thinks my husband is a murderer. Kelsey gives me a tiny smile, though, and once more, I'm relieved to think there's yet another person who hasn't decided I should be run out of town on a rail.

"I'm okay. You look like you're hiding out back here. Everything okay?"

Once more, I try to decipher from the look on her face and the tone of her voice if she knows anything, but I'm not getting the feeling she's about to tell me she thinks I'm scum. How quickly that's become something I expect.

"Well…you know how it is. Sometimes the day just gets to you," I answer, knowing all too well it's not even ten o'clock in the morning yet.

She nods like she understands, but she couldn't. It's nice that she's trying, though.

"Give me a minute or two, and I'll come back and we can talk about it. Today's already been a tough one for me, so I'm grabbing an extra-large. Be right back!"

With that, she walks up to the counter and orders her food while I stare at the door to watch for every person who's coming in. Maybe I shouldn't have come here today. I should have done the drive-thru and gone home.

Every horrible thing that could possibly happen plays out in my mind, only interrupted by Kelsey returning to the table to join me. I force a smile because I don't want her to know I'm utterly miserable, but she seems to be able to see right through my happy façade to find the truth.

After taking the first bite of her hot, buttered scone and then a sip of her coffee, she folds her hands in front of her and says, "So, I get the feeling something's wrong. I know we don't really know one another very well, so I understand that you might not want to talk about it with me. Just know that I've got two really strong shoulders and two ears happy to listen to what you have to say."

Ordinarily, I wouldn't tell anyone I've only known for such a short time what's bothering me, but I almost can't stop myself. If I don't get to talk to someone about this, I'm going to end up hiding out under the covers for the rest of the day.

I take a big gulp of my iced latte to give me courage and start to tell her what's happened. Kelsey listens as I explain how Connor went out while I was taking care of all the girls at the party and something terrible happened. Then I tell her how the kids at school are shunning my daughters while the mothers are acting like I'm the worst person in the world. I barely keep myself from crying the entire time, but I get the whole story out, thankfully.

It's too much for me, though, when she reaches across the table and gently pats my hand. Her kindness makes my emotions surge to the surface, and before I know it, I'm sobbing in the back corner of The Coffee Mug.

"I'm sorry," I mumble from behind my hands. "I guess I'm just very emotional today."

"Oh, Jamie, it's okay. Cry away. Don't stop on my behalf. Sometimes a good cry is the best medicine for what ails you."

I wipe the tears from my face and try to be strong, even if I feel like I'm going to fall apart again at any moment. "I know. I just need to be strong for my daughters and Connor, but when it's just me, I swear I want to just cry my eyes out. I've worked so hard to give my girls everything they could need to be successful, and in one weekend, it's all been smashed to pieces."

"Well, you know your husband better than anyone else, so if you say he wouldn't do anything like that, then that's good enough for me."

She sounds so sure of herself when she says that. The problem is I don't feel that sure about what she's claiming. I've never seen Connor get violent with anyone, but he does keep guns in the house, so he isn't completely against hurting another person.

After a minute or so of my not saying anything, she leans in and quietly asks, "Is it possible? You didn't say anything when I said that, which makes me think there's something else on your mind."

Immediately, I shake my head no. "Connor isn't a criminal. If I believed that for even a split second, I'd go to the house, pack up my things and the girls' things, and leave him today."

Again, she nods. "Okay, then. That being settled, now the police just need to catch up with what you know. Have they questioned you at all? Maybe if they heard that from you it could help."

"No, they haven't talked to me at all. I'm guessing they figure since I wasn't there that I wouldn't know anything that would help the case."

That I might know something isn't wrong, but that it's a detail that could hurt my husband is a problem.

Kelsey seems to pick up on my apprehension about Connor and says, "If you tell me anything, I promise I won't tell a soul. Trust me. I know how it feels to be involved in something you had no part in starting."

Maybe it would be okay to tell her and only her. She has been very nice.

I lean close to the table and whisper, "I don't know if this is important, but when I checked my husband's storage box for his guns yesterday, one was missing. I thought the police would figure that out by now, but nobody's mentioned that at all. They're all talking about him being a murderer, and they don't even know one of his guns is missing. If they knew, I can only imagine what they'd say."

Knowing that makes my stomach clench from stress. All of these people we considered friends of ours already believe Connor is a killer. Just wait until the cops find out one of his guns is gone.

"Forget them, Jamie. People love to gossip. I swear it's the most popular thing in suburbia. The gun being gone is concerning, though. You don't think he had that gun on him when he went for the hike with that poor man, do you?"

I want to shake my head. I want to definitively say there's no chance in this world that Connor would have taken a gun with him on a simple hike around our community. I don't think I've ever seen him do anything with any of the guns he owns.

But I can't say without a shadow of a doubt he didn't have that gun on him Saturday.

Quietly, I give voice to the worst thing I've ever thought about Connor. "Kelsey, I don't know. Why would he take a gun on what was basically a nature walk?"

She shrugs and shakes her head. "I don't know. I'm not from around here, so maybe he thought there may be some wild animals he'd see that he might need protection from?"

Even as she says that, I see she doesn't believe it any more than I do.

"Wild animals on what's basically a trail in a park? We all call it a hiking trail, but the HOA handles the upkeep, so it's not like it's exactly a wild area. Oh, God! What was he thinking?"

Suddenly, my emotions get the better of me, and I begin sobbing quietly again. Am I saying I think Connor possibly used his gun to kill that poor man? I don't know. All I do know is none of this looks like it's going to get better anytime soon, and that means I have to figure out what I'm going to do to protect my girls.

As if she's reading my mind, Kelsey says, "Maybe you should take your daughters away for a little while. Can you go to a relative's house to visit? You wouldn't have to tell them why you're going away. It can just be a little trip out of town."

I think about that for only a second before I know I can't. "No, the girls have their big meet coming up next week. They can't miss practice at all before that."

While I'm telling her that, all I can think about is the team shunning Cassandra and Danielle just like those kids at school did. Neither one said yesterday's practice was bad in that way, but the longer this mess goes on, the bigger the chance is that even with as talented as they are, gymnastics is going to be ruined by the horrible rumors going around about their father.

Damn Connor! I could just scream when I think about what this is doing to our children.

Worry settles into Kelsey's expression, making her mouth turn down so lines form. Added to her scars that are ever present, they show how worried she is about me.

"I know what I'm about to say is unnerving, but hear me out. If you believe your husband is innocent, maybe you should tell the police about his gun being missing. They'll do a ballistics test on the gun they found at the scene, and hopefully, that will clear him."

As much as I know that sounds like a good idea, I don't know if I can do it. "What if it turns out to be his gun?"

Kelsey sighs. "That would be bad."

When I don't say anything, she asks, "So you do think there's even the tiniest possibility that he could have done this?"

I can't bring myself to answer her. All I can do is nod, and even that feels like a betrayal of my husband.

She sets her jaw and nods like she knows what will fix this for me. "Then I believe you have to think about yourself and your girls now, Jamie."

I start to defend Connor, so she quickly says, "I'm not saying you shouldn't stand by him. I'm just saying your daughters need you to protect them now. People can be very cruel. Your girls did nothing wrong, but you know how things go. Children overhear their parents talking, and although they may not understand what's going on, they follow their parents' lead. It's wrong, but it happens. I don't want to see you or your daughters hurt by this."

She's right. I know she is. But abandoning Connor isn't something I'm prepared to do. We may have had our ups and downs over the years, but he's my husband.

I belong at his side, just as our daughters do.

Kelsey gives my hand a sympathetic pat and then writes something on her napkin. Handing it to me, she says, "If you ever need me and I'm not here, just call that number, okay?"

I smile, thankful for a friend in this horrible time. "I appreciate that. I worry things are going to get worse before they get better, so I just might be calling."

"Good. I told you before. I have two good ears to listen to whatever you need to talk about, so call whenever you need to."

CHAPTER THIRTEEN

 onnor

I RUB THE LAST OF WHATEVER SLEEP I GOT AFTER coming home from the police station from my face and roll out of bed. After dealing with Tweedle Dee and Tweedle Dum last night, I made sure to call Martin to tell him I couldn't come in today. Checking my phone, I see he texted and he's fine with my being out today.

At least that's one good thing to happen to me lately.

Clinging to that and wishing today would be better than yesterday, I make my way downstairs to grab some breakfast. The house is quiet, thank God, so at least there's that.

I don't dare spend any time on my phone checking the news like I usually do each morning. I can't bear reading about how I'm the only suspect and everyone around here is convinced I'm guilty.

What has my life become?

My peace is shattered when I hear Jamie walk in the front door. Not a minute later, she walks past me into the kitchen, mumbling something. I know I shouldn't ask what she's saying, but the words are out of my mouth before I know it.

"What are you saying?"

She throws me a nasty look and shakes her head. "Nothing. Nothing at all."

As much as I don't want to have this conversation, it's either now or later, and to be honest, I'd like to get it over with. I stand up from the table and walk over to where she's standing at the island in the kitchen, sure she wants to get this over with as much as I do.

"I didn't kill him, Jamie. My God. He shot himself. You believe me, don't you?"

My wife gives me a blank stare and then sighs. "You were the last one with him. That's what they're saying. The last person to see him alive."

That's all she says. Not that she believes I could never hurt anyone, much less kill a man. Not that she's behind me when the rest of the world wants to lock me in prison and throw away the key.

No, all she can talk about is what everyone is saying.

"Because we were hiking! You can't just believe in me, can you? Jesus, you've known me for over fifteen years," I say in disbelief that my own wife isn't standing by me on this.

She remains silent, so I say the words I never thought would leave my mouth. "You think I did it."

"I think people are going to talk, Connor. They already are. The girls told me kids at school were saying you're a murderer. The mothers at gymnastics acted like I was a criminal myself. They looked right at me with such disgust. Right through me. Like I was diseased."

"So that's it? You're not worried about me? That I'm being framed for murder? You're worried about the girls' social standing at gymnastics?" I ask in utter disbelief.

What happened to our vows that said we'd love each other through better and worse? The first time we hit a rocky patch, she's eager to throw it all away, and for what? People liking her and the girls being popular?

"You think this is about social standing? Do you know what it's like to watch our daughters ask why everyone is talking about their father? Why people are saying he's a killer? Jesus, Connor. You're not the only one hurting here."

I'm not sure I want the answer, but I need to ask. "And what did you say to them? What did you tell our daughters?"

Her voice cracking, she answers, "I lied. I said it's a mistake. That you'd never hurt anyone. That everything was fine. But it's not fine, Connor! The police came here to our house."

"Because I was with him when he shot himself. How many times do I have to tell you? I couldn't do that. You know me. I'm not a killer. It's crazy!"

With each word, my voice grows louder until I'm almost screaming at her. Jesus, this is so frustrating! Jamie knows me. She knows I couldn't kill Bryan. I barely knew the guy. What reason would I have for wanting him dead?

We stand there in the brand new kitchen she said she had to have, complete with top of the line stainless steel appliances better suited to a professional kitchen than a suburban one, and there's only one question on my mind now. It's the most important question I've ever asked her.

"Do you believe me when I say I didn't kill him?"

My heart slams in my chest, and I swear that's all I can hear as I stare at her and wait for her answer. Bryan's death has turned my life into a nightmare, and it's only getting worse by the minute.

Jamie frowns and answers, "I don't know what to believe! You won't even tell me what happened up there!"

"I've told you everything there is to tell. Bryan and I were up on the hiking trail, and he grabbed my gun. I assumed he knew what the hell he was doing, but he started waving it around. I told him to stop so we could get going on our hike, but then the next thing I knew, the gun went off and he was on the ground. That's it. That's all there is to tell."

She looks like she's about to cry when she says, "So you did take your gun. Why? What did you need a gun for? You were going for a damn walk, Connor!"

I shrug, wishing I never even had the idea to grab my gun before I left that day. "I don't know. I can't tell you why. I just did. But I swear I didn't shoot him."

"Then why are they saying you did it? Suicide and murder aren't similar at all. I watch those crime shows on TV, so I know. The angle of the shot would be all wrong if they're saying it's murder when he really shot himself."

I close my eyes to try to find some bit of patience. "I know. I've thought the same thing a million times. I told those idiot cops that, but they've already tried and convicted me for this."

For the first time, Jamie looks relieved. "Well, then that's it then. We just have to wait for the coroner to clear all of this up."

If only it was that easy.

Shaking my head, I say, "He already determined it's homicide. I don't know what kind of person they have in that job, but if it's anyone like those two morons Ramon and Raintree, I have to think this town needs a better person in that position."

Jamie's expression twists into one of horror. "He already said it's not suicide? How? He's the coroner, Connor! They know about these things. If he said it's homicide…"

Her sentence trails off as if she can't bring herself to say the words. I grab her hand, afraid if I don't that she'll leave. I have to know she's on my side in all of this. I don't know what I'm going to do is she abandons me.

"I went up there the other night and someone hit me on the back of the head. I was out for hours lying on the ground until the cops found me at one in the morning. I think someone is framing for this, Jamie. It's the only thing that makes sense."

She gives my hand a squeeze as she shakes her head. "What is going on, Connor? Who would follow you up on the hiking path and attack you like that?"

"I don't know. The cops found me, and of course, they don't believe a word I'm saying. Those two wouldn't know a damn clue if it crawled up their asses."

Jamie gently takes her hand away from mine and walks over to the sink. After splashing water on her face, she dries off with a dish towel and turns around to face me.

"Did you see anyone else that day? Anyone at all? It's usually busy on the weekends up on those trails, isn't it? One time Danielle and I went for a walk up there, and I swear it was like we were on a pilgrimage with all those people."

God, I wish I could tell her what she wants to hear. I'd love for it to be true too.

"No, not a soul. It was strange. There are always people up there, but when Bryan and I got up to the clearing at the top of the first little hill, there wasn't a soul around. I don't know where the hell everyone was. He mentioned he thought they could be down on the golf course. Then we talked about how that wasn't possible since there wasn't a reservation open for the next few weeks."

Waving her hands, she shakes her head wildly. "Forget all of that nonsense! It's not helping. We need to focus on the difference between suicide and murder. That coroner is the one who will save you. Maybe he just needs some more time to look into it."

"No! He already decided it wasn't suicide. How the hell would I even be able to make him see he should take a second look?"

Sadly, she has no answer to that. Nobody does. That's the problem. If the coroner had at least said Bryan's manner of death was undetermined, that would make it possible for me to argue my case. He didn't. He took one look at the damn body and decided it was homicide.

And now I'm public enemy number one.

Jamie's silence is deafening. I always thought that if I ever ran into trouble with anything in life that she'd be by my side supporting me one hundred percent. What I see in her at this moment says that belief was wrong.

"The cops say I should hire a lawyer. If I have to, we're going to have to cut back on some things around here."

I watch as her reaction tells me everything I need to know. Her eyes get big, and she looks like she's about to cry.

"Like what? We're barely spending on anything now, Connor. What are you planning to cut out?"

Looking around where we stand, I say, "Well, we can get rid of those streaming channels. We can cut back on the landscaper to once a month, and we can handle the upkeep of the yard."

"Once a month! Our yard is going to start looking like a jungle if we only have him come once a month," she says in that voice of hers that's nothing but pure whining.

"Then we'll have to mow our lawn ourselves, Jamie. It's not like it's all hills and hard to do."

She narrows her eyes in anger and asks, "And I assume you think I should do it since you work full-time?"

I'm in a fight for my life, and she's only concerned with how much effort she'll have to put into the goddamned lawn! How did I ever think she would stand by me when times got tough?

"I assume you're going to do your part, Jamie. And if the lawyer costs as much as I think he will, then the girls are going to have to stop their gymnastics lessons. At least until everything is cleared."

My wife backs away with a look of pure disgust like

I've just informed her of some horrible secret she can't respect. It's fucking gymnastics! Am I supposed to keep paying for those damned lessons instead of paying for a lawyer?

"Connor, I won't let you do that to the girls. They've made the team. They're fantastic gymnasts. I won't let your mistake ruin their chances for scholarships and college. I won't."

Something inside my brain snaps, and I bark, "My mistake? I went for a walk with a co-worker! That's it. That's my mistake. If you want them to stay in gymnastics, then you better find a job because that's the only way we'll be able to afford it if I have to hire a lawyer."

She glares at me for that. Sorry, honey, but tough times call for tough measures.

Jamie points her finger at me as she continues to glare in my direction. "When we had Cassandra, we decided I would stay home. Then when the girls went to school all day, I wanted to get a job. You said no. Now, after all these years, you want me to get a job? Yeah, that's going to be easy."

Everything is about her. Why can't she just support me?

"Nobody is saying you'll have to get anything professional when it comes to a job. Just something that will help now. Get something that will allow you to use the skills you use here. Maybe a short order cook or a waitress."

Her face twists into an ugly expression. "I manage everything in this house, although it's clear you think that's not much if you think I should just get a job as a cook or a server. I drive the girls wherever they have to go. School. Gymnastics. Social events. Me. I'm the one who shuttles them around, not you. I do all the cooking and cleaning here. I do all the shopping. I make sure all the bills are paid on time. I handle everything here. Anything that has to happen around this house happens because of me, and now you say I should get a job if I want the girls to stay in gymnastics? Maybe if you had agreed to my getting a job when Danielle went to first grade we wouldn't be in such a hard place now."

I've heard enough out of her today. If she can't support me, then I don't need to bother with her anymore.

"You may do all of that, Jamie, but there would be no house, no private school, no gymnastics, no landscaper, and no anything else without me. Remember that when you're listing all the things you do around here."

As I push past her, she says, "I don't know what to do. I don't know how to keep them safe from this... this nightmare. The looks. The questions. The police coming to the door."

I spin around and look at her in disbelief. "Maybe stand by me? I am your husband. Anyway, they don't have evidence, and they need that to actually bring charges. A good lawyer would be able to rip that idiot coroner's report to shreds."

Except a good lawyer is going to be almost impossible to afford since we're practically living paycheck to paycheck as it is.

"They don't need evidence. They need a narrative. And right now, the story they're telling makes sense.

Hiking trip. Coworkers. Jealousy. Just wait until everyone finds out it was your gun."

I look at my wife like I don't even know her because it feels like I don't right now. "Do you hear yourself? Jealousy? Jealous of what exactly, Jamie? Bryan and I had the same exact job at the same company."

"I don't know how many times I've heard you complain that your boss always gives him preferential treatment at the office. I doubt I'm the only person you've ever said that to, so all they have to do is find one other person who will say they heard you say those things about him."

Frustrated, I try to keep my calm, but I want to scream. She can't even support me in the tiniest way.

"You don't believe me, do you? I thought of all people you'd know I'm innocent of this. I thought I could at least count on you being on my side."

That makes her expression soften, and she sighs like she's got the weight of the world on her shoulders. "I *am* on your side. I'm on *our* side. But I need to know the truth, Connor. Because if it comes out in court, in public, and I've been lying to our girls…"

"You want the truth? Then here it is. I didn't kill him. I was his friend. We worked together. I wish I hadn't agreed to go hiking with him that day. I wish I hadn't gone at all. I wish I hadn't taken the gun with me. I wish I'd stopped him when he took the gun out of my hand. I wish I'd done something different. Everything different. But I didn't kill him."

I stop, take a deep breath, and then say, "Just tell me you believe me. Tell me you're with me on this."

Jamie is silent for a long time, but I don't leave. I

need to hear her say she's with me on this. We've never been tested in this way before in our marriage. I've heard every couple is severely tested at least once in their years together. Well, this is it, and there's only one answer to give me.

Finally, she says in quiet voice, "I'm your wife, Connor. I'm with you. I just need you to know I have to protect the girls too."

I don't say anything to that because that sounds a lot like she's not standing with me. I consider saying I want to protect the girls too, but the truth is I have to think of myself now.

If I don't, then there may not be an us after the police are done.

CHAPTER FOURTEEN

amie

I DON'T KNOW WHAT TO DO. I LOVE MY HUSBAND AND want to support him in his time of need, but what am I going to do to protect our daughters? They're the ones who will suffer most from these horrible rumors about their father.

Connor paces through the living room, so I walk upstairs to our bedroom. I can't stand it when he's like this. My husband doesn't do well with stress. It turns him into a man I barely recognize, and I know if I stay downstairs that we'll end up having a fight.

When I reach the top of the stairs, my gaze is drawn to the girls' rooms. I make my way to Cassandra's room, which is right next to ours, and smile at the pink walls she absolutely had to have. We spent two weeks picking out the exact shade she wanted, going to three home improvement stores before we found one that had the perfect color of pale pink. She, Danielle, and I spent a weekend painting her room, and when we finished, I was so proud of my daughters.

My mind drifts back to the moment we moved all her furniture back in and began to hang her posters on the walls. She couldn't wait for me to hang her shelf so she could display her first medal from gymnastics. Cassandra fussed over that gold disk for nearly twenty minutes before stepping back and proudly showing me how great it looked in the middle of the shelf. Ever since, whenever she wins or places in the top three at any meet, she carefully places her prize on her special shelf.

As soon as Danielle saw her sister had a beautiful, new pink room, she had to have hers painted. A different child from her older sister, my second daughter wanted a purple room. Danielle has always been more regal than Cassandra, so that color fit her perfectly. Again, it took a while for us to find the exact shade she loved, but once she settled on a beautiful lilac color, she couldn't wait to paint her room. Just as we did with her sister's room, the three of us spent a weekend making her room perfect for her. And like her sister, she too had to have a shelf for her awards.

As I stand in the doorway of Cassandra's room looking at that shelf full of her achievements, I can't imagine telling them the sport they love and do so well at is going to have to cease to be a part of their lives. How can I do that to them?

I think that and know I can't. I won't betray them like that. They do their best every day at practice and at every meet. The least I can do is make sure they can continue to enjoy gymnastics.

God, how did our lives turn into this? Just a week ago, my girls were the stars of their team, and I was one of the mothers who knew she didn't have to hover at every practice to ensure they'd get their chance. Now people are whispering behind our backs, and Connor may be arrested soon for murder.

My worry makes my stress level inch up, and I know I can't stay in this house. I need to get out and get some fresh air for a while. I don't have to pick up the girls from school for a few hours, so I have a little time to compose myself before I have to see them again.

Where can I go, though? I don't want to run into anyone from the community or any of the mothers from gymnastics, so all my usual places are out. Even thinking that makes my stomach twist into a knot.

Now I'm avoiding going to spots I love.

Worry morphs into anger, and I spin on my heel to storm back down the stairs. I don't know where I'm going or what I'm doing, but I have to get out of here.

As I march through the living room, Connor stops pacing and asks, "Where are you going?"

I don't look at him, focused on just getting the hell out of my own house. "I don't know. I'll be back later."

And with that, I leave him standing next to that ugly chair he loves likely wondering why I'm not staying home. I may run into some ugly looks and whispers from people, but I can't stay cooped up today.

I avoid looking at any of the houses around mine as I head to my car, unable to face the stares from neighbors I've had at my house for parties and barbeques on holidays. Slamming the driver's side door, I sit staring at the pale green garage door for a long time as I try to figure out where I can go.

Sure there's nowhere to go and I'm going to spend the afternoon sitting in my car, I suddenly remember Kelsey gave me her phone number. Maybe she won't mind me meeting me somewhere.

I text her and sit back in the driver's seat, my eyes closed while I wait for her to text back. Thankfully, she only takes a few minutes and suggests a different coffee shop than my usual one close to her house. A quick glance at the name and her directions and I'm ready to go.

As I drive down my street, Anthony Ricci stands on his porch putting up his American flag, and I instinctively wave like I always do. I watch as he turns away without returning the wave, my stomach sick over it. When his sister came to visit him last summer and wanted to see the area, I was more than happy to chauffeur her around for an entire day while he spent time with his brother-in-law. I was good enough to be his friend then, but now it seems I'm not even worth a tiny wave.

So much for the HOA's motto: Many neighbors, one big welcoming community. I guess that's just lip service to make potential homeowners think the people here are nice. Nobody better ask me to contribute to a damn thing for the next community day.

I stew about Anthony and that ridiculous HOA the

whole way to Cuppa Cuppa, the coffee shop near where Kelsey lives. I've seen this place once or twice, but because it's out of the way on my usual drive, I've never stopped here.

God, I hope nobody from gymnastics or from my neighborhood is here.

As I walk toward the door, I think to myself that I've never been this nervous walking into any place before. This is what my life has turned into. Now I'm someone who worries wherever I go.

I hold my breath in anticipation of who I might see inside, but when I walk in and see only Kelsey sitting at a table in the back, I let out a heavy sigh of relief. Hurrying back to join her, I collapse in a chair on the opposite side of where she's seated.

"Hey, are you okay? You looked like you were going to be sick when you were standing up near the door," she says sweetly.

Nodding, I force a smile. "Rough day. I'll be okay once I get something in my stomach. How's the coffee here? Any suggestions for me? I've never been here."

Kelsey gives me a broad smile. "Oh, it's pretty good. About the same as the other place. The scones are even better here, so don't miss out on them."

I take a deep breath in and let it out slowly before standing up. "Okay, need anything while I'm up there?"

She waves me off and shakes her head. "No, I'm good. I'll be here."

Five minutes later, I return to our table with my large, iced coffee and a cranberry-orange scone heated with butter. Kelsey points at it and smiles.

"I'm so glad you're not having to eat dry scones anymore. The cranberry scones here are to die for!"

The moment I hear that word die I cringe. I don't mean to, but hearing anything about death today is too much for me.

"Everything okay, Jamie? Didn't you want to get a scone?"

All of a sudden, I can barely contain my emotions. I want to scream and then cry and then have someone take me in their arms and give me the biggest hug I've ever had. Tears stream down my cheeks, and before I know it, I'm in a full-blown meltdown.

Kelsey reaches across the table and gives my forearm a gentle squeeze. "Jamie, honey, what's happening? This can't be about the scone."

God, now I'm truly losing it in a coffee shop. I don't know if I can take much more of this.

I dry my eyes and compose myself before I lean closer to her and whisper, "I'm sorry. This whole thing with Connor is wearing on me. I didn't mean to break down like that."

Concern fills her eyes. "Has anything happened? The last time we spoke, you were worried about the gun that killed the man being your husband's. Did you find out something?"

The way she hits at the most crucial point strikes me as so insightful, and yet it shows Kelsey is caring because she clearly listened to what I was saying. I'm not used to that from friends. None of the mothers at gymnastics actually listen to what anyone is saying, including me. Talking is for finding out things about people, not to hear about someone's life.

Lowering my gaze to look at my scone with the dots of orange and red sprinkled through it, I admit the terrible truth. "He said he took his gun on the hike and that Bryan grabbed the gun out of his hand and was waving it around when he accidentally shot himself."

The words come rushing out like they're desperately in search of someone to understand them. When I look up, I see my new friend comprehends perfectly what I'm saying.

Before she can say a word, my emotions begin to unravel. "Oh, God! What am I going to do? My neighbors won't even look at me. The mothers at gymnastics were whispering about me and my family, and the kids at my daughters' school are saying their father is a murderer! It's like you're the only friend I have now. I don't know what to do."

"Shhh…it's going to be okay. I know it doesn't feel like it is right now, but I can promise you everything will be okay. Remember, I know something about having your world crumble around you."

Kelsey points at her cheek where the deepest scar exists, and I nod, so utterly thankful that someone understands what I'm going through. I don't know how I got this lucky at the very time I need it most, but if I didn't have her to talk to, I don't know what I would do.

"How did you handle it? I don't think I'm strong enough."

I've never been that brutally honest with how I'm feeling a day in my life. I don't know why, but something about Kelsey makes me feel like I can truly be myself.

She smiles, and for a few seconds, the scars that mar

her beautiful face become less invisible. They never fully disappear, though.

"It took me a long time to come to grips with what happened. I didn't want to go on living for a long time. If it wasn't for my friends, I don't think I would have been strong enough to make it through. So just like they helped me, I'm here to help you. Whatever you need, just let me know. If you just want to talk things out, I'm hear to listen. If you want me to take you somewhere, just point the way. Whatever you need, say the word and I'm on it. That's what my friends did for me in my time of need, so that's what I'm doing for you."

I love how kind she is. I don't know what I did to deserve her, but right now, all I can do is thank God she's my friend.

"Sort of paying it forward?" I ask with a chuckle which must seem completely opposed to the sadness practically etched into my face nowadays.

"Exactly! That's the way to do it. We're all in this together, Jamie. We've all got things we have to deal with. When they get too hard to handle on our own, that's when friends step in and help. Tell me what you need, and I'll be on it like white on rice. My grandmother used to say that. I don't exactly what it means, but it seems right for this occasion, doesn't it?"

As she takes a sip of her drink, I think about that odd saying she used and how I know it because of Connor. "That's so strange. My husband says that too. I'd never heard it before I met him, and he said his grandfather used to say it all the time."

Kelsey nods, and her smile gets bigger. "It's a very

small world, I guess. Now tell me how to put a smile back on your face."

"I don't know. I feel like my entire world has been upended by this. I can't wrap my brain around the idea that Connor could hurt someone, much less kill anyone. He says it was an accident, but the coroner says it's homicide."

As soon as that word leaves my lips, I look around to make sure no one is close enough to hear me. I still can't believe my life includes that horrible word.

"I told him the coroner would be able to see that the angle of the gunshot would show it's suicide, that Bryan shot himself. He may not have intended to do that, but it happened that way and not the way the coroner currently claims it did. But what if he doesn't see that? What if the police find out it was Connor's gun? Then nobody is going to believe it was an accidental suicide."

Once more, Kelsey gently gives my forearm a squeeze. "You can't worry yourself about that. Science is science, Jamie. If that gunshot can be proven to show it was a suicide, then any decent lawyer will be able to find a specialist who can attest to that. I'd say your husband has nothing to worry about if he can rely on the science to prove him innocent."

She's trying to be helpful, but the mere mention of Connor needing a lawyer to get out of this mess only makes me sick to my stomach. Lawyers cost money. Great lawyers, the kind that can find the right specialists to testify to the angle of the gunshot being evidence of suicide, not murder, cost a fortune.

"That's the thing. He's already told me that we can't afford a lawyer." I stop and cover my face with my hands. "What am I going to do? Connor's talking about not paying for the girls' gymnastics because we have to pay for a lawyer."

"It'll be okay. I promise it will. I know it feels like that's impossible right now, but look at me. I'm living proof that you just have to believe things are going to work out."

I drop my hands and sigh. "I think I'm going to have to get a job. As much as I want to be there for the girls whenever they need me, I have to find a way to pay for their gymnastics. That means the world to them. I won't force them to give them up."

Kelsey nods and then asks, "Do you have any relatives you could stay with for a while? This situation with your husband is obviously wearing on you, and I don't think you're going to be able to find a job if you're feeling this way. At least if you didn't have to worry so much and could get away from the problem for a little while, you could at least get some breathing room."

She's trying to be supportive, but the very idea of leaving Connor to deal with this whole thing on his own feels wrong. I'm his wife. I'm supposed to be there in sickness and in health, till death do we part. That's what we said in our marriage vows, and until this horrible mess happened, I never doubted I was the kind of woman who lived up to every vow she made.

Now I wonder if I can and still protect my girls the way they need me to.

"I'm so torn, Kelsey. I don't want to abandon Connor when he needs me most. On the other hand, I can't think being surrounded by all of this awful situation is good for my daughters. I don't know what to do."

"Oh, I completely understand, honey, but your daughters are innocent bystanders to all of this. You're right to be concerned about their well-being. That's just you being a good mother."

I do want to be that for my girls. That's all I've ever wanted is to be the best mother I can be for them. It's why I spent every afternoon being front and center at their gymnastics practices. I wanted to make sure the coach knew the Jennings girls had someone in their corner. I didn't want them to be children who had no one watching out for them while all the other girls had their mothers making sure they weren't overlooked.

For a few moments, I think about how we could go to my parents' house. It's only about thirty minutes away, and since I'm happy to drive the girls to and from school like I always do and to and from their practices, it wouldn't be much different. They'd get to keep their daily routine just as it is.

After I finish my scone, I take a drink of my iced latte. Kelsey's right. Whatever I do, I'm doing it out of my sole interest to be a good mother to Cassandra and Danielle.

"I think I'm going to ask my parents if we can stay with them for a little while."

That gets me a big smile from Kelsey. "That's a good idea. I think a little space from all the chaos will be all you need to protect your daughters."

She's right. I know that. I guess I just needed a friend to spell it out for me.

"The girls will be able to stay at their school and with their team, so it's not like their entire lives will be uprooted. I just hope they understand."

"Oh, I bet they understand far more than you think. That's why getting them away from all of this will be good for them. Plus, I'm sure you three spending time with your parents will be great for everyone."

I nod, sure my parents will be thrilled to get a visit from us. The girls adore their grandparents. I bet that will be just what they need.

Hopefully, Connor will understand why I have to do this.

 onnor

JAMIE PACES PAST ME AS I WALK THROUGH THE FRONT door, her left arm flailing in front of her as she listens to someone who must be upsetting her on her phone. Probably another of those mothers who don't want to let their kids come over here to hang out with the girls because they're convinced the gossip is right and I'm a murderer.

I don't try to talk to her because I don't want to hear any more whining about how our girls' social lives are being ruined and how I need to do something to fix it. I'm trying. She has no idea how much I want this to all go away.

Maybe I should let her complain to the cops. Maybe Larry and Moe will enjoy listening to her bitch about it.

It would serve them right if I sent her down there right now. At least I'd get some peace and quiet.

I don't make it halfway to the stairs before she asks, "Where have you been? It's nearly four o'clock. You've been gone for hours! I was calling all over looking for you."

Waving her off, I shake my head and answer, "I was out. I couldn't stand being in this house anymore. Not that going out is much better. Good old Tony, the man who's never been shy about borrowing every damn power tool I own, gave me a death stare as I was driving past his house before. All I want to do is rest now."

Her eyes open wide like I just said the most ridiculous thing a man could say at this moment. "You can't rest! Our lives have been turned upside down in the past few days, and you want to rest? No, Connor. We need to discuss what's going on."

I stop walking and close my eyes in the hope that if I can't see her, then I can't hear her either. Unfortunately, that's not how it works, and even though I'm able to block out the vision of Jamie frantically waving her arms around in a panic, I still have to listen to her.

When I finally look at her again, she seems like she's about to explode. I'd love it if I had a supportive spouse at this moment. Someone to stand by me and assure me we were going to get through whatever happened.

So much for that.

"I don't want to discuss what's going on anymore, Jamie. I don't want to discuss anything. Nothing at all. I just want to go upstairs and hope to wake up tomorrow morning to a world that hasn't gone fucking crazy!"

My outburst makes her take a step back, and for the

briefest of moments, I have the hope that she finally understands that now is not the time to have any kind of discussion with me. That hope is dashed a second later when she shakes her head and starts talking again.

"I'm thinking of taking the girls to my parents' house for a few days" she says with tears in her eyes.

Her words hit me like a sledgehammer to the center of my chest. She's going to take my girls away because she thinks I'm a murderer.

"What? Why? Don't you believe in me, Jamie? Now you want to take my children away from me? Don't I have enough horrible shit going on in my life?"

Instead of looking at me, she averts her gaze and stares down at her feet or the floor. "I just think the girls don't deserve to have to deal with this."

Fucking terrific! My entire life is falling apart, and now my family is abandoning me.

Grabbing my wife by the shoulders, I fight the urge to shake her until she understands what this is all doing to me. "No, I won't let you do this! I didn't kill Bryan. What do I have to do to make you understand that?"

She stuns me when she pushes me hard in the chest, sending me stumbling back until I hit the sofa table. "Don't you dare put this on me! I didn't take a goddamned gun on a hike for some stupid reason. You think the girls and I should have to suffer through this with you? Why? We didn't do anything wrong, yet nobody wants to talk to us anymore and we get people staring and whispering when we walk past them. How is that fair, Connor? Tell me! How is that fair?"

"Fairness has nothing to do with this. It was an accident, Jamie. How many goddamned times do I have to say that? That idiot coroner is wrong. I don't know why they can't tell the difference between a suicide and a homicide, but until they do, I'm going to keep protesting my innocence because I didn't do it!"

The two of us stare at one another, both of us surprised. Our marriage hasn't been one of constant fights, so we aren't used to screaming at one another. I don't think I've raised my voice to my wife five times in the fifteen years we've been married. Jamie and I aren't excitable people, so it's like neither one of us knows how to handle this terrible mistake.

We both take a few moments to calm down, and when she finally speaks again, her voice has returned to its usual sweetness. "Connor, I have to think about the girls. They're suffering too, you know. It won't be for long, and my parents' house isn't far. You can see them whenever you're free."

She barely gets those words out before I'm livid again. So now I get to pay a mortgage for a house I never wanted but my wife insisted on? I bet she thinks I should still keep footing the bill for those damn gymnastics lessons too.

"I can't believe you're doing this to me. How are you better than that asshole Tony who suddenly thinks he's superior to us but had no problem being a mooch with every tool I own ever since he moved into this goddamned neighborhood? What are people going to say when they see you aren't around? Anyone who doesn't know us is going to think that's proof of my guilt. I thought I knew you better than that, Jamie."

My attempt to guilt her into staying fails instantly, and I see by the flash of anger in her eyes she's not going to take any blame here. "You thought you knew me better? I feel like I don't know you at all, Connor! You go out with some guy, and he ends up dead. Everyone says you killed him. I don't know if you did or you didn't, but I won't let those beautiful girls of ours have their lives ruined because of some stupid mistake!"

I rush at her and grab her by the shoulders, shaking them to get some sense into her. "How can you say that? You don't know if I'm a murderer? What the hell is happening to you?"

Her eyes grow big as she shakes her head frantically. "How can I say that? It's like I don't even know you anymore. You're not the man I fell in love with."

"What does that mean? I'm the same person I've always been. I can't believe you don't know if I'm guilty of killing a man."

The room feels like it's closing in on me as I say those words. I drop my hands from her arms, releasing her. She doesn't know me anymore? Why? I'm the same person I've always been with her. I go to work every day. I pay for every damn thing her little heart desires. How can she say she doesn't know me anymore?

Jamie doesn't answer my question, which tells me everything I need to know. My own wife doesn't believe me when I say I didn't shoot Bryan. It's as if nothing that's happened between us for the past fifteen years of our marriage matters to her. We hit one tiny bump in the road, and all she can think of is bailing on all we have together.

"Fine. Go! I don't care. Leave me when I need you most. But I won't let you claim it's because of our daughters. You're doing this because you're a coward,

Jamie. Yeah, a coward. I've given you everything you've ever wanted from the day we married, and when I need one thing, you're nowhere to be found."

That makes her find her voice again, and she takes a step closer to me so we're practically toe-to-toe with one another. I feel her warm breath as she stares up into my eyes with such rage that I can't imagine she ever loved me.

"Don't you dare make it seem like this was all one-sided, and you gave so much while I did nothing. I'm the reason this house looks as nice as it does. Since you don't seem to remember, let me remind you that this house needed updates throughout. I wanted to call people who knew how to fix what needed to be fixed, paint, and make this house as nice as it could be, but all you ever did was complain about money and how much you couldn't afford it. You, Connor. Not us. Not our family. You. So I'm the one who handled the painting and designing everything here. Every other woman I know can call people to fix things, but no! I had to learn how to fix a toilet that won't stop running and a sink that won't stop dripping."

God, this woman is insane if she thinks that means anything in the big scheme of things.

I shake my head in disbelief that she's talking about fucking paint colors while I'm talking about life and death issues. "You always have been entitled, Jamie. You want. That's all that's ever mattered. What you wanted."

Her anger radiates off her in waves now as she screams, "Entitled? Are you kidding? Who's the person who made sure this house was good enough for your boss and your coworkers from the office to come by and be impressed? Not you. That's for damn sure. And who has made every meal since the day we moved in here? On top of that, I've washed your clothes, cleaned the house, paid the bills, shuttled our children everywhere they need to go, and made sure all you had to do was go to work. Everything else has been handled for you, Connor, so don't you dare stand there and call me entitled!"

She makes it sound like she's the one who's been doing all the heavy lifting around here. I go to work five days a week, fifty weeks out of the year. For every year we've been married, I've done my duty as a husband. Yet, she acts like that's not enough.

I'm done talking to her about this. She's made up her mind, so now I have to decide what to do.

Turning on my heel, I start walking toward the stairs. "I'm sorry you had it so tough all these years, Jamie. I hope you find a better life at your parents' house. Good to know who's in your corner in times like this."

Behind me, she says in a small voice, "It doesn't have to be forever, Connor. Why can't you understand the girls don't deserve to be caught up in this madness?"

When I look back, I don't see the woman I stood before God, our family, and our friends to pledge to love and cherish one another forever. All I see is a stranger I thought gave a damn about me.

Now I know I was wrong.

CHAPTER SIXTEEN

onnor

I WAKE UP AND SEE IT'S ALREADY DARK OUT. I'M alone in the bed I've shared with Jamie for fifteen years, and then suddenly all that happened between us this afternoon comes rushing back to me. She's not here because she doesn't believe me.

She's taking my kids away because she thinks I'm a murderer.

Part of me believes this has to be a nightmare I can wake up from, but I'm not asleep. I don't understand how this is happening. I agreed to go for a walk with a coworker. That's it.

If only Bryan hadn't been so stupid as to wave that gun around so carelessly.

They say hard times show you who your real friends are. It seems I don't have a single friend to stand by me.

Martin said he didn't believe I was guilty, but he had to be nice like that. Martin is a softie. He couldn't be mean to someone if you paid him.

I thought I could count on those I love, but Jamie showed me that isn't true either. She and the girls are all I have. My parents are dead, and I haven't spoken to my brother in over a decade after he fell off the wagon for the fifth time. I couldn't keep letting him around the girls when he was drunk, and he was always three sheets to the wind.

So I have no one.

As that harsh reality settles into my brain, I hear knocking downstairs. Maybe it's Jamie and the girls. If she forgot her house key, she'd have to knock.

I jump out of bed and hurry downstairs in just my shorts I wore when I crawled under the covers to take a nap. As much as I should be angry with my wife, I can forgive her. I need her by my side during this time. Jamie and the girls believing in me is all I need, so I don't care why she's back.

I'm just happy she's realized by my side is where she should be.

Without looking through the peephole, I fling the door open ready to show her how thrilled I am they decided to stay, but my hopes are dashed when I see Officers Ramon and Raintree standing on my front porch. I don't think I can hate two people more, so having to see them and their judgmental stares only serves to make me want to slam the door in the faces.

"Mr. Jennings, we're here to speak to you. Do you have some time now?" Officer Ramon asks in that officious voice he likes to use whenever he sees me.

I don't answer for a few seconds as I try to regroup from my disappointment at not seeing Jamie and my girls. Talking to these two assholes is the last thing I want to do tonight. They've already chosen to not do their jobs and focus solely on me, so why would I bother?

"Not tonight, gentlemen. I'm busy. Have a nice night."

Just as I'm about to enjoy slamming the door in both of their faces, Raintree says in a voice that's nothing short of gloating, "We know the gun that shot Bryan Corsei was yours, Mr. Jennings. Why didn't you tell us that before?"

My fingers grip the edge of my front door as my mind whirls with fear. They know. They know the gun was mine. Now I won't have a choice but to hire a lawyer. Even if that moron coroner decides to actually try using scientific methods and figures out it was suicide, they'll still look at me for bringing the gun.

I swallow hard and answer Officer Raintree's question. "Because I didn't kill anyone. If I had mentioned the gun was mine, you wouldn't even have considered anyone else, not that you have. You've spent all your time assuming I'm the one who shot Bryan, but I'll tell you for the hundredth time, it wasn't me! Now leave me alone!"

This time I do slam the door in their faces, but it doesn't feel as good as I'd anticipated because my mind is full of the reality that there's no way I can avoid paying a lawyer now. I lean against the door while I try to figure out what to do, and from outside I hear Officer Raintree speaking to me.

"Mr. Jennings, you have the chance right now to tell us all that happened. The prosecutor may be able to help you, but if you refuse to speak to us, we'll have no choice but to assume you're guilty."

Although I know I shouldn't, my frustration with these cops gets the best of me, and I fling the door open again to say, "You've been assuming I'm guilty from the moment you arrived at the community center. I told you someone had been shot, and that barely registered on your radar. You took your own sweet time walking up to where Bryan was, and he may have lived if you two hadn't dragged your fucking heels the whole time. His death is your fault, no one else's, so go home and sit with that for a while. The next time you come here you better have a warrant because if you don't, I'm not talking to you ever again."

Officer Ramon starts to say something, but I'm not listening to him. I shut the door and lock it before walking back up to the bedroom. I slide under the covers and close my eyes, unable to believe this is my life now.

My mind drifts back to the last time the police thought they had me for a crime. It feels like another lifetime ago, but as soon as I think about it, all that happened comes rushing back to me.

"Connor, answer the door!" my mother yells from the basement where she's folding clothes.

I want to say I'm busy, but I know what will happen if I do that. She'll lecture me on how I don't pay rent here, even though I turned eighteen months ago, so the least I can do is help her out with things like answering the door.

Begrudgingly, I trudge to the front door and open it to see a policeman standing in front of me on our brick porch. My blood feels like it stops flowing through my veins for a few seconds, but I force myself to smile so the cop doesn't know how nervous I am right now.

I don't say a word, so the officer with the badge that says Miller and a big read nose that screams he's a drunk clears his throat and says, "Son, are you Connor Jennings?"

My kneejerk reaction is to tell him I'm not his son, but I don't. All I do is nod, sure I remember watching some TV show that said the less you say to the cops, the better.

"Is that a yes, that you're Connor Jennings?" he asks, and this time the question has a little edge to it.

"Do you want to speak to my mom?" I ask, happy to push him off on her.

"No, I want to speak to you. Now once again, are you Connor Jennings?"

And again, I nod but still give him nothing more.

His frustration shows when his gray, bushy eyebrows draw in toward that red, meaty, bulbous nose. Even as I think that, I can't believe I used bulbous in an actual, real world sentence. Mrs. Anderson from senior English would be so proud. Actually, knowing that old bag, she'd probably give me a shrug if I told her. She always was a pain in the ass.

"Son, the police are investigating a death in the woods last night over near Shaney's Mountain. Do you know anything about that?"

I shake my head and smile. He wouldn't be asking me if he thought he had me dead to rights. I'm no dummy. I've seen Law and Order. True, it was only because I was grounded for a month in tenth grade for getting into a fight after school with that shithead Brett Kolino, but I paid attention when I had to sit with my mother and watch TV during my incarceration.

"Perhaps it would be a good idea for me to speak to your parents. You said your mother is at home? Please get her for me."

Officer Miller looks downright irritated because I refuse to speak to him, and even though I'd like to piss him off more, I figure letting my mother deal with him is probably the best plan. I bet he decides he liked my silence better than talking to her, though.

I take my time walking to her room where she's busy hanging clean clothes. She's been in a bad mood all night, so the last thing I want to do is spend any time with her. This little visit from our town's finest is going to make her even more miserable.

She is better than Officer Miller, though.

"Mom, there's a cop at the front door who wants to talk to you," I say as I stand in the doorway to her bedroom.

She looks over at me before hanging a navy blue T-shirt on a hanger to go in her closet. I tell her T-shirts are supposed to be folded, but she claims that leaves them wrinkled. Hanging them up like she does is just weird.

"What does he want?" she asks in a rushed way, already telling me she's not happy having to deal with the cops tonight.

Not that anyone is ever happy to have to deal with them.

I shrug. "Don't know. I didn't talk to him."

My mother stops hanging her shirts and levels her gaze on me, narrowing her eyes as if she's trying to figure out if I did anything wrong to bring the police here. Dressed in a white sweatshirt and gray sweatpants, she straightens her clothes and lets out an unhappy groan.

"This better not be about something you did," she warns as she walks past me.

Curious about what Officer Miller is going to say to her, I follow my mother to the end of the hall and stop there to eavesdrop on their conversation. She walks up to the front door but doesn't *offer to let him come in. I come by my distrust of cops naturally, it seems.*

"What can I do for you, officer?" she asks him, and even though the words sound like she's trying to be nice, anyone who knows my mother can hear her irritation that she has to speak to him at all come through loud and clear.

Through the screen door, he says, "Ma'am, we're investigating a death in the woods last night. We were wondering if your son could give us any information regarding it. We've been told he and some of his friends were there around the time the death occurred."

My mother looks back in my direction and then turns back to face the cop. "My son was home with me all last night. I'm afraid he won't be able to help you. Sorry."

And with that, she closes the door and marches over to where I'm hiding. Pointing her figure at my face, she says, "You better not have done anything stupid. If you and your friends were around when it happened, then you and your friends need to get your stories straight. Got it?"

I nod but say nothing. Rich and Mike know nothing about what happened last night, but they'll be good if they find out about everything. They're not going to rat me out. We know what it's like with the police around here. They only protect and serve the side of town where the big houses are. Down here in The Patch, they think we're all fucking criminals at birth. So we keep our mouths shut whenever they come around asking their questions.

Since they won't protect us, we protect our own.

The memory of the cop's visit to my house fades, and once again I'm alone in my bed, safe and sound.

For now.

CHAPTER SEVENTEEN

amie

I'VE NEVER FELT MORE EXPOSED IN MY LIFE. I'VE SAT in my car parked in this exact same spot hundreds of times before, but today, I feel like all eyes are on me. I'm probably just being paranoid. This thing with Connor has me sure every person I encounter is judging me.

That's crazy, though. What is that thing people always say? Dance like no one is looking because they're not? Is that it? I can't remember, but I'm sure that axiom is more right than wrong. People have their own things going on. Why would they care to focus on me?

Anyway, I'm sure this whole thing is about to die down. It's been nearly four days, after all. Yesterday was likely the climax of the insanity. From now on, things will calm down.

Even as I think that, I know better. The police are going to find out that was Connor's gun that killed Bryan. Once they realize that, it's only a matter of time before they arrest him.

A slight drizzle begins to fall as I sit outside the gym waiting for the girls, so thankfully, I have a justification for not walking over to stand with the other mothers today. I can see them from where I'm parked, though, and each one of them has looked over at me more than once. Every time I waved, and not once did anyone wave back. Instead, they turned up their noses and ignored me.

To think that I considered these people my friends. Guess I was wrong on that call. Friends stand by you in times of trouble. After all the hours I've spent with these women, someone I know for barely a week turns out to be a truer friend than any of these people.

Some might think me stupid for believing these women were my friends. I guess it was foolish. All we have in common are our daughters and their love of gymnastics. Still, I thought we would always be civil to one another. How many times have I taken care packages to their homes when I heard they were sick? How many times have I welcomed them and their daughters to my home? More than I want to count and look what being nice got me.

Being practically shunned for some rumor about my husband that hasn't even been shown to be true.

I can handle it. It hurts, but I'll survive. It's my daughters who don't understand why other children are saying cruel things about their father and why their parents aren't kind to them like they used to be.

The rain hitting my windshield becomes heavier, and the mothers all run for cover to avoid getting wet. It's not much, but I'll take that tiny bit of satisfaction from seeing them scurry into the building so their perfectly coiffed hair doesn't get ruined. I see Jasmine Rey didn't make it in time, so that lovely three hundred dollar hairdo she loves to brag about looks like a wet rat on top of her head.

A song I haven't heard in nearly fifteen years comes on, so I turn it up and close my eyes. Memories of my freshman year in college come back to me, and I can't stop myself from remembering the night I met Connor.

It was a warm spring night, and my sorority sisters and I were celebrating passing all our finals. I was going to be spending the summer in town to take a social psychology class I needed for my minor. My parents had agreed to pay to let me stay at school for summer courses if and only if I earned a B in every one of my spring semester classes. I was sure I'd aced all my finals, but the only one I absolutely needed to pass with at least an eighty was my statistics class. Never terribly good with numbers, that single course had threatened every plan I had made, but I crammed for that test for over a week, ignoring everything but classes to study day and night.

My mind quickly switches to my friends in the sorority and where they all are now. We all swore we'd keep in touch and never forget one another, but those promises fell by the wayside when real life got in the way. Marriages to our spouses, births of our children, careers, and a million other things conspired to make us strangers.

I thought I'd be best friends with those girls forever.

How long has it been since I spoke to anyone from college? I've been out of school for over a decade, and I can't remember the last time I talked with any of my sorority sisters.

Sad about that, I try to enjoy the song since it was popular back when Connor and I first got together. He didn't attend the same college as I did, but that night he was in the neighborhood near the sorority house for a party at one of the fraternities. He got bored and wandered out into the street, and a car nearly ran him over. Drunk with his reaction time slowed, he could have been killed by that driver, but he somehow stumbled out of the way, falling to the ground next to my friends and me on the sidewalk.

It's not a wonderful story of how we met. It's certainly no meet cute. He was drunk, and I had enjoyed a few beers before leaving the house myself, but those were different times. I'll never forget the first thing he said to me.

"Any chance you've got a smoke?" he said with a devil-may-care smile as he looked up at me from where he lay on the sidewalk. "I figure since I just cheated death that I should at least do something to celebrate."

I told him no since I didn't smoke, and when my friends urged me to keep walking since we were late to the frat party already, I stayed with him. I told myself I was worried he might mistakenly walk into the street again and get hurt, but the truth was Connor had a way about him that charmed me.

Maybe it was a type of meet cute after all.

He likes to say it was a typical middle class couple meeting, which sounds much less interesting than the actual story, but that's Connor. He doesn't like to romanticize anything. He likes to say, "The plain truth is the best, Jamie. Anything else is just a lie."

I've always thought of my husband as a truthful man. In fact, until recently, I would have said he was a man who wouldn't tell a lie about anything.

These past few days have made me question that claim. What really happened up on that path? I don't understand why he took a gun in the first place, but why did he take it out and let Bryan grab a hold of it? None of that sounds like Connor.

I see the first girls coming out the front doors of the gym and looking around through the downpour for their mothers' cars. My girls aren't out yet, so I hang back and don't get in the pick up line. One by one, I see my daughters' teammates leave while I wait for Cassandra and Danielle. The coach must have asked them to stay. I hope all this terrible nonsense with Connor isn't affecting their gymnastics. They were so thrilled to have made the team.

That was just two weeks ago. How quickly life changes.

When all the cars leave, I see Vanessa's daughter standing alone with no sign of her mother. I start my car and drive up to the front of the building before lowering the passenger side window. Allie sees me but doesn't smile or wave, so I call out, "Honey, do you need a ride? I'm happy to take you home as soon as the girls come out."

She turns to face me, and I instantly see she looks uneasy. Slowly, the rain begins to slow down, so she walks over to the car and leans in.

"I'm sorry, Mrs. Jennings, but I'm not supposed to talk to you."

I know the reason why, but still I have to ask. "Why?"

She hangs her head and in a low voice says, "My mother says I can't. I'm sorry."

"Okay. Hurry back under the awning so you don't get wet, honey."

I sound chipper as I say that, but inside, I'm crushed. If she's being like this with an adult, I have no doubt she wasn't any friendlier to my girls. My heart feels like it's in a vice someone twists tighter and tighter when I think about them being shunned.

A car pulls up behind me, and I look in the rearview mirror to see Vanessa Dennis behind the wheel. She doesn't wave or smile. She simply gives me a look that says she doesn't like me anymore.

I look away, unable to deal with the rejection from the one person who has the power to help. I thought talking to her would stave off any repercussions from what's happening with Connor. I guess I was wrong.

As she drives past my car, I can feel her stare. It's ugly and hateful, but I keep my gaze focused on the touchscreen that says a song from Madonna is playing on the radio. I wouldn't know. I can't hear anything right now but my heartbeat in my ears.

Finally, I look up when I know she's gone and see my daughters slowly walking out of the building. Their expressions tell me they experienced the same thing I just did, and once again, my heart clenches in my chest.

I paste a smile on my face and honk the horn. They run over to the car, and for a second, I let myself believe

I was misreading what I was seeing. Maybe things weren't as bad as I'm making them out to be. True, kids can be cruel, but gymnastics is a team sport, so they all have to work together to do their best.

Cassandra and Danielle pile into the back seat of my car and slam the door shut. Ordinarily, they talk a million miles a minute about school and practice. I can barely keep up on most days.

Today is not like that. They sit silently not even speaking to one another. I don't know what happened at practice, and I'm a little afraid to ask.

But I have to know.

I put the car in drive and casually ask with a big smile, "How was practice? Did you hit that vault you've been working on, Danielle?"

Silence.

When I brake to stop before pulling out onto the street, I look up at the rearview mirror. Both the girls are crying.

"Hey, what's going on? Did something happen at practice?" I ask, my fear at what I'm going to hear growing by the second.

My younger daughter can't stop sobbing, but Cassandra answers, "Nobody would talk to us, Mom. It was horrible! Thank God we have each other because they wouldn't even practice with us. Coach said he was going to have a team meeting tomorrow, so maybe they'll be better after that, but today was terrible."

My instinct as a mother is to protect my girls, and I have to fight the overwhelming urge to turn this car around and march right into the gym to ask the coach why the meeting has to wait until tomorrow. What the hell was wrong with setting those girls straight today? What kind of coach lets two girls be hurt under their watch?

"I'm sorry, honey. I'm sure it will be better once Coach Mark talks to everyone."

Those words taste like ash, but I have to say them. What I really want to do is drive to each of those girls' homes and tell their parents what I think of them and the way they've been treating my family.

As I drive, I wonder how to broach going to my parents' house for a little while. Maybe they'll be happy to have a break from the house. A change of scenery is always nice.

When I hear Danielle sniffle, I say, "What would you think about going to see your grandparents? I was thinking we'd go visit for a little bit."

Immediately, Cassandra asks, "But what about gymnastics? After coach talks to everyone tomorrow, things will be okay again. We have a big meet next week. We have to be there for it, Mom."

"Oh, not to worry. I'll be driving you back and forth to school and practice, so everything will stay the same. We'll just be staying at Grandma and Grandpa's. That'll be fun, right? They have a pool, and there's that ice cream shop a few blocks away that you love."

As hard as I'm trying to sell this abrupt change, my daughters remain silent. I need to convince them, or every moment we're at my parents' house will be misery. Let me see. What did they love the last time we went there?

After a few seconds, it comes to me. My father took

them to that trampoline park the last time, and that's all they could talk about for days afterward.

"What about that great place Grandpa took you to? You two loved that place. You said it was the most fun you ever had."

For the life of me, I can't remember the name. Thankfully, my description is enough, and Danielle squeals from the back seat, "Oh, Jump! I loved that place! Can we go there if we go to Grandma and Grandpa's?"

Cassandra starts getting excited too, and before long, both of them are talking about how much they can't wait to go to the trampoline park. I haven't seen them this happy in ages. Thank God for that trampoline park. That will make having to leave home for a while much easier.

Then my younger daughter asks me a question that makes all their happiness immediately disappear. "Daddy's coming with us, right?"

I force myself to smile when I look back at her in the rearview mirror as I stop the car at a red light. "I think he's pretty busy at work, but you never know. Daddy sure does love to surprise us, so it could happen."

Everything about my tone is wrong as I speak. I'm too happy. Too perky. Too up considering what's happening to our family right now. All I can hope is my girls don't pick up on it.

Thankfully, they're too involved in talking about how much they can't wait to go to the trampoline park to truly understand what I'm really feeling. All the better. They don't deserve to have to deal with any of what's going on. It's bad enough they've had to endure the taunts of children at school and at gymnastics practice over what's happening with their father.

Now I just have one final hurdle to overcome before we leave.

"Mom, when are we going to Grandma and Grandpa's?" Cassandra asks. "Can we go today?"

I know she means the trampoline park more than her grandparents' house, but I'm just glad they're taking this news as well as they are. "Actually, we're going to go home and pack, and then we'll set off for their house."

My daughters laugh and start planning on what tricks they want to try when they go to the park. Thank God children are resilient. I've been dealing with the same treatment they're getting from their classmates and teammates, and I'm not handling it anywhere as well as they are. I wish I could be as easily distracted by a couple hours of jumping on a trampoline.

By the time we reach our house, they're so excited they bound out of the car into the house. I follow them, noticing on my way up the sidewalk to my front door that Mrs. Campbell across the street is standing on her porch glaring at me. What did I ever do to her to warrant this? Last year when her furnace went out during that cold snap and the repairman couldn't come out for three days while she had to say in a freezing house, who cooked her hot meals and brought her a space heater and blankets? Nobody else in the neighborhood but me, and yet now when there's talk about my husband possibly killing that poor man, she looks at me like I'm a criminal.

So much for innocent until proven guilty.

I see Connor immediately as I walk in the house, and as soon as my gaze falls on him, I know this mess has taken its toll. The dark circles under his eyes give away that he hasn't slept well in days. Never a truly good looking man, he's always had a look about him that showed he was fun. That's gone now, replaced by worry that appears to have been permanently etched into his face.

"The girls told me you're taking them to your parents' house and to some park they like. Is it an amusement park or something?"

I study the confusion in his eyes and realize he has no idea what park they're so excited about, even though they and I told him all about it as soon as we came home last summer. They raved for days about every flip and jump they performed that afternoon.

Does he ever listen to us when we talk to him?

As I walk past him into the kitchen to get a drink of iced tea, I answer, "No, it's a trampoline park, Connor. You should know this."

Behind me, he says, "I've been a little preoccupied with other things lately, Jamie."

I don't want to have a fight right now, but his ignorance about everyone but himself suddenly makes me want to scream. I struggle to keep my temper under control, silently telling myself there's nothing to be gained by an argument.

"It's a trampoline park. My father took them the last time we were there to visit. Remember, last summer when you were too busy to come with us?"

"Don't start, Jamie. I had to work. Not all of us get to just flit around and come and go as we please. Some of us have to work a job to pay for everything."

I don't know if it's his snotty tone of voice or his

bringing up that I don't work again, even though he was the one who insisted I be a stay-at-home mother once the girls were born. Maybe it's just that I'm sick and tired of being a social pariah because of my dear husband. Whatever it is about him right now, I'm tired of everything about this man.

Spinning around to face him, I snap, "Don't start? Well, I have an idea. How about I finish? I'm taking the girls to my parents' for a while. I don't know how long. You're welcome to come visit as often as you like, but since you've only been to their house once in the entire fifteen years we've been married, let's just say I'm not making any bets on you actually showing up. That's entirely up to you. I'm sure your daughters would love to see you. As for me, I'm done being the reason you're miserable, Connor. What's happened to you is because of you and no one else. Go live with that for a while."

He says something about how I should be supporting him in his time of need, but I'm not listening anymore. I have a bag to pack and the girls' clothes to get ready to go to my parents' house. I don't have time to listen to him complain.

Those days are over.

CHAPTER EIGHTEEN

onnor

THE WARM SMELL OF A FIRE SOMEWHERE NEARBY FILLS the air as Mike, Rich, and I make our way to our usual spot to hang out and drink in the woods near the high school. The cops never come up here, which always amazes me since nobody makes it a secret that we all party in this place. Maybe the police just don't care. It's not like we're doing anything wrong. We're just having a few beers and some laughs. What's wrong with that? So what if we're underage? The whole having to be twenty-one to drink is stupid. They can send us to war, but we can't have a beer? Ridiculous.

"Did you see that girl at the convenient store?" Rich

asks as we head down the path. "I've never seen her around here before."

Mike laughs at our usually timid friend. "Yeah, I saw her. She must be new around here, or I would have noticed her already."

With more than a hint of dejection in his voice, Rich mumbles, "Noticed her? You would have banged her already."

I laugh at his disgust with our friend's success when it comes to girls. Out of the three of us, Mike always gets whoever he wants while Rich and I end up wishing we were as ballsy as he is. Girls love his confidence, something the two of us are sorely lacking, unfortunately.

They don't mind his six foot three height too, something neither of us can claim to have. Son of a bitch had a growth spurt in seventh grade and never seemed to stop. Rich and I have never caught up, and by the way our health teacher talks, the possibility that either of us will ever top six foot is highly unlikely now.

I guess we'll have to hope we can find some girls who like their guys around five foot ten. It's only a few inches. Other than that, all the two of us have to work on is our confidence. In that area, at least I have something going for me. I'm no Mike, but I can fake it pretty much most of the time, especially once I've got a few beers in me. Poor Rich is too damn shy and usually can't even approach girls, no matter how much he's had to drink.

Mike looks over at Rich and smiles. "Well, don't sound so upset, dude. I saw you checking her out and told her and her friend to come up here and join us. By the way, their names are Samantha and Kelsey. Samantha's the one you liked."

When I glance over at Rich, I see his face lit up with a huge grin. Mike can be a complete dick when it comes to girls most of the time, but if he's not interested in one, he's happy to help a friend out. Neither Rich nor I like to admit it, but we're happy to have him do the work to get girls to come around.

By the time we reach our usual spot in the woods, all I can think of is popping open a beer and chugging it down. We sit on the rocks we arranged around a campfire a while back, and Rich proceeds to hand out the refreshments for the evening.

Raising his in the air, he smiles and says, "To having a great night after a shitty week of school."

Mike and I raise our bottles to his toast before pounding down our first beers in a matter of seconds. Rich takes a little more time, but after a minute or so, he's onto his second one too.

"Can you believe old Mrs. Loftus giving me a hard time?" Mike asks, shaking his head before he lets out a loud belch. "That old bitch doesn't want to see me graduate, you know that? I swear to God if she fails me for the quarter, I'm going to find a way to make her last days on earth a living hell. I promise you that."

"What can she do? It's not like they're going to hold you back. You're a senior. Nobody ever fails senior year," I say with a chuckle.

"That's what she threatened me with last Monday when I was late to class again. I can't help it her damn speech class is right after homeroom. Who the hell needs speech class anyway? I obviously know how to speak."

The three of us laugh at that comment before Rich mimics Mrs. Loftus and her famous words she says to us nearly every damn time we have speech day. "You must annunciate!" he says in a shaky voice that sounds just like the old bag's when she barks at us while we're up in front of the class. "Annunciate, Michael!"

"I'm going to annunciate. All over her damn face. Bitch," Mike grumbles.

Reaching over to grab his third beer, he looks at Rich and me and silently asks if we need another. The two of us shake our heads. Rich always ends up nursing his drinks, but tonight I'm thinking he's going slow for the same reason I am—if we're going to get laid, we need to at least be able to function. Pounding down half a dozen beers before those girls get here is going to make getting it up difficult, even for two eighteen-year-old guys who have hard-ons almost constantly.

The three of us sit in silence for a few minutes as the smell of burnt wood begins to dissipate. Whoever had the campfire nearby must have left. That means we're probably the only people out here in the woods tonight.

Good. The last thing a guy needs is some stranger walking up on him while he's trying to get into some girl's pants.

These woods are usually filled with people during the warmer months, but once school starts up again, the crowds thin out. The first sign of a chill in the air makes everyone head indoors for their fun, but we like to hang out here as long as we can. Last year, we even drank a few times when there was snow on the ground. It was a little cold, but we had a cooler all around us, so at least the beers didn't get warm.

"So when did the girls say they'd come?" Rich asks eagerly.

Damn. He must really like that Samantha chick.

I laugh as Mike looks over at him, and in the moonlight, I can see he's amused too. "Soon. Jesus, Rich. Desperate much?"

"Fuck you. I'm not desperate. I just asked a simple question. You don't have to be such a dick all the time, Mike."

He tips the bottle back and downs the last few ounces of his second beer before tossing it off to the side. Things always get edgy between these two when it comes to girls. Maybe if Mike didn't seem to get every damn one he laid his eyes on, Rich wouldn't get so fucking surly about him busting his balls about them. I don't know how he does it, but I swear Mike is a chick magnet.

He elbows Rich in the side and chuckles. "Sorry. I was just having a little fun. Samantha told me she and her friend had to meet up with someone before they could get up here. I think they were buying some weed or something. I'm sure they'll be here soon."

Rich just shrugs and gives him a half-hearted smirk. This is how things usually are until Mike gets so blasted that he starts telling both of us how much he loves us and how much he thanks God for having friends like the two of us. It's a little sappy, but he means well.

At least he's not a mean drunk.

Hoping to get the two of them talking again, I grab my third beer and say, "Did you see the signups for the winter dance in the cafeteria at lunch today? That Laura Carollton was manning the table. Too bad she's stuck like fucking glue to that idiot boyfriend of hers. I'd go to a dance with her."

Rich and Mike look over at me like I've just announced I'm going to be moving to Neptune next month. They stare at me for a long moment before Mike finally says, "You have a thing for homecoming queens? I had no idea, Connor."

"Yeah, I mean, you've never mentioned her even once before, and now you're saying you'd go to some dumb dance just for her?" Rich says like he's shocked I could even notice someone like Laura.

"I don't have a thing for her or any other homecoming queen. I've noticed her. Don't tell me you haven't. She's fucking gorgeous, for Christ's sake," I say, suddenly feeling defensive about liking the hottest girl in school.

That makes Mike throw his head back and laugh. "Of course, I've noticed her. I'm not fucking dead. But Jesus, Connor. She's been with Chase the asshole star quarterback for so long I figured nobody even paid attention to her anymore. I mean, there's taken and then there's Laura Carollton taken. They're probably talking about their impending wedding plans right now."

"Yeah, Connor. She's so into him it's like she can't see he's a total tool," Rich says with a chuckle. "Not that she's not hot, but like Mike said, she's so taken there's no point in even looking at her."

"Doesn't mean I can't notice her and think I'd do her."

It's not that they're wrong. Laura Carollton is Chase's. Nobody's saying otherwise. But Jeez, can't a guy dream?

As I sit there on that cold rock fantasizing about what it would be like to be with her, Samantha and Kelsey call out from the path, "Hey, you guys out here?"

They sound unsure, like they think we're the kind of asshole guys who'd say we're going to be partying in the woods but bailed, leaving them out here alone. Obviously, they don't know us. We're not the type to leave once the beers have started.

"Over here!" Mike yells.

I see Rich look over toward the path and watch the current girl of his dreams as she and her friend walk over to join us. She smiles in his direction when she sits down on the rock next to him, so he has a good chance of getting together with her tonight. The other one sits down next to me, strangely enough. I was sure she'd be more interested in Mike. Girls always are.

"What's up?" he asks, taking on the role of host in the absence of any female attention on him. "Want a beer?"

Both girls say yes, and it doesn't take long before we're all laughing about some story Mike tells about the last time we were out here and he got so damn drunk he pissed himself over in the bushes. Like usual, he's the center of attention, but for one of the rare times in our friendship, Rich and I got the girls.

Samantha seems to really be into Rich, and a short time after she and her friend join us, those two pair off and walk away to be alone. Kelsey and I listen to Mike tell another story about something his parents did when they all went away on vacation to Dollywood last summer, and when he gets to the part where his father thought some guy in drag was Dolly Parton and he ran up to him and gave the guy a big hug, we all laugh until our sides hurt.

Truly enjoying the memory, he leans back and falls onto the leaves covering the ground. Kelsey and I look over to see that he's okay, and I give his leg a push.

"Mike? You good?" I ask, secretly hoping he stays down there so I can get some alone time with this girl.

"Mmm...good. I'm just going to rest here for a minute," he says in a drunken voice before passing out.

Kelsey giggles and then smiles at me. "I think your friend is toast."

"Yeah, but that's a good thing, don't you think?"

Not exactly my smoothest line, but it will have to do. She seems pretty willing anyway, so unless I grow another head or start rambling about having a doll collection I spend hours dressing up, I think I should be good to go.

I take her hand and guide her away from drunken Mike and in the opposite direction from where Rich and Samantha are so we can have some privacy. Kelsey holds onto me tightly as we climb over rotting logs and rocks left behind when other people moved them to have their own firepit.

"Do you know your way around here?" she asks right before she trips over a huge rock.

I catch her and answer her question. "Yeah, don't worry. I've got you."

We walk for about five minutes before I remember I didn't grab more beers for us. Damn! Oh, well. If I'm lucky, I won't be drinking much in the next hour or so anyway.

I finally find a place that isn't too hilly or too littered

with rotting logs and stones too big to move. We sit down on the ground to get comfortable, and Kelsey says something about wishing we had a blanket. It's not a bad idea, but I wasn't planning on getting laid tonight.

That right there is the difference between Mike and me. He's always planning on getting some whenever he leaves his house. For me, it's like the damn stars have to line up perfectly, and even then it's not a sure thing.

But tonight it's going to happen. If anything or anyone dares to get in my way, I swear I'm going to gut them.

I get busy sliding my hands under Kelsey's jacket and find a sweater, another shirt underneath, and finally a bra. Was she planning on playing a game of strip poker tonight? No matter. I find what I'm looking for and tilt my hips to press my already hard dick against the front of her jeans to let her know I'm ready to go.

Just as I'm burrowing under the waistband of her jeans, I hear a crunching noise like someone walking over dry leaves. Annoyed, I look up expecting to see Mike or even Rich if he struck out already with his girl, but instead I see some old guy watching us like some goddamned pervert.

"Who's there?" he asks in a way that tells me he thinks he owns these fucking woods.

Kelsey hurries to cover herself as I silently admit I want to kill this guy for interrupting us. What the hell is he doing out here in the dark? Who takes a walk in the woods at ten o'clock at night?

"Go away!" I bark, hoping to get back to what Kelsey and I were doing up until a few seconds ago.

"You're trespassing. I'm going to call the cops."

I open my mouth to tell him to fuck off, but he turns and walks away. Call the cops? On two adults having a little fun in the woods? Fucking asshole.

"What the hell is wrong with him?" I ask as I roll off Kelsey and sit up to see where he went to.

"It's okay. He's just some old guy. Probably has nothing better to do with his time than come out here to look for people having a good time. I doubt he's going to call anyone, and even if he does, I doubt the cops will come. I know in my town you have to be bleeding or be waving a gun around like a maniac to get the cops to do anything."

I nod, knowing she's right. He can call the goddamned cops all he wants. It's a Friday night during football season. The cops in this town have a lot more important things to deal with than coming out to break up two people having sex in the woods.

But it still pisses me off.

I move to stand up and follow him, but Kelsey grabs my hand. "Don't bother. It's not worth getting all upset about. He's gone now."

As much as I know she's right, that shit he pulled still bugs me. He better not call the cops. I swear if he does I'm going to find out where he lives and show him how big a mistake that was.

Kelsey tugs on my arm to pull me down on top of her and kisses me. "Forget him. I'm right here."

She's right. She's here, and I have a good chance of getting some. I can leave that asshole until later.

CHAPTER NINETEEN

onnor

My rage won't fade, even though that guy left and I have Kelsey right here, ready and willing to do whatever I want. She's got her hands all over me, yet all I can think about is that asshole threatening to call the cops.

Son of a bitch acts like we're doing anything wrong out here. Old fuck. He's probably just jealous because he doesn't have anyone who wants to touch his shriveled up dick tonight.

Kelsey's fingers rake through my hair as I kiss her, something that normally gets me excited since I have a thing with my head being touched by a girl. Tonight, though, it's not working.

Goddamned bastard! First he interrupts us, and now

he's the reason I won't be getting any tonight. If I ever run into him again, he better watch himself. Payback is a bitch.

I lean back away from her and then sit on the ground, wishing I could just clear my damn head so we could get back to the good stuff. Beside me, she sits up and sets her hand on my thigh. Christ, usually that would really get me going, but even that isn't working tonight.

"Hey, what's wrong? I know you were having a good time. I could feel it against my leg," she says quietly, her cheek resting against my shoulder.

"Nothing. Sorry. That guy just really pissed me off. Who the hell does he think he is? We're not doing anything wrong or even anything illegal. Why come out here in the middle of the night looking for problems? If that's what he wants, I'll give him one."

Kelsey snuggles up against me and says in a soft voice, "Forget him. He's probably some lonely old guy who misses his golden days when he had fun. Of course, back then it was in the rumble seat of a Model T."

She giggles at her attempt at a joke, but I can't find any humor in me at this moment. That guy needs to learn it's not cool to ruin a person's night because you're a miserable old bastard.

I struggle to stand up while Kelsey tugs on my arm to keep me there with her, but all I can think about now is teaching that guy a lesson. Ripping my hand from her hold, I glance down at her and see I've ruined my last chance with her tonight.

"Where are you going? I thought we were having fun," she says in disgust as she gathers up her clothes.

"I need to take care of this. That guy is going to learn I'm not the person to fuck around with tonight."

"Well, what the hell am I supposed to do? Just sit here and wait for you?"

With a shrug, I answer, "Do whatever you want. I'll be back in a little bit. If you're here, good. If not, whatever."

As I set off to find that old guy, behind me she curses me out for being an asshole like she thought I might be. Too bad. We could have had a nice time if it wasn't for someone rudely interrupting us.

"I'm not waiting here, Connor. Just so you know," she calls after me, like she's trying to punish me for leaving.

I wave off her comments as I focus on making it back to the main path so I can find that asshole. He headed toward the road, so that's where I'm going. If I'm lucky, I won't have to follow him all the way back to his house since I don't know where he lives. I'm guessing it's in one of those houses right where we parked tonight before walking into the woods. He probably hates anyone who does that because they're going to have a good time, and he can't stand that.

Shithead. I can't wait to show him he screwed with the wrong guy tonight.

I see a figure ahead of me, but I can't tell if it's him or not. It looks like this person is the same height as the guy, but I don't want to go jumping some tall chick by mistake. I break into a jog to catch up to whoever that is, but a few seconds later, I see them turn around and it's not who I'm looking for.

Dammit! I can't lose that guy.

I run past the person in the dark and focus on finding my way to the street. He's already home by now, I bet. That's what I get for staying with Kelsey.

By the time I reach the edge of the woods, I see the guy I want. He hasn't reached his house yet, thankfully. I sprint up behind him and grab him around the neck to take him by surprise. He lets out one tiny, frightened cry, but a second later, I've got him down on the ground. I jump on top of him and stare down into his eyes so he knows it's me, the guy whose night he ruined.

His face is a mess of wrinkles, and around his mouth the lines from always frowning are the deepest. Just as I suspected, he's a miserable fuck who's always ruining things for others.

Pinning his shoulders to the ground, I grunt out, "How's it feel, asshole? Couldn't just leave me and the girl alone, could you?"

He mumbles something, but I don't understand him in my rage. I've never been this angry in my life. I swear to God I could kill this man.

I squeeze my right hand into a tight fist and cock my arm back, and then it's like the rest of the world suddenly fades away, leaving only the two of us in the world. He looks up at me with horror in his eyes but doesn't try to stop me as my hand comes down toward his face. My fist connects with his nose, breaking it instantly. Blood spurts everywhere as he shakes his head back in forth in agony, spraying blood across his cheeks.

The second punch comes fast, right after the first one, but this time my fist smashes into his cheekbone. It's like every ounce of rage I possess is being channeled into my hand, so when it hits him, it sounds like a heavy thud.

For the first time, he tries to stop me. With his left hand free, he swats at my face to make me stop, but it's no use. I'm blinded by the need to teach him the lesson of not fucking with me. He cries out when I pound my fist into his face for a third time, but the sound seems far away and muffled, like he's underwater screaming at me.

I couldn't stop now if I wanted to, and not a single cell in my body wishes this was over. I feel powerful, and with every time I hit his face, that feeling grows exponentially. I'm not even sure the strongest man in the world could pull me off him right now. I'm like some kind of superhero with powers no mere mortal can withstand. I've never felt like this before. It's better than anything I've ever felt before in my life!

Over and over, I slam my fist into his face. At some point, he stops crying out and then a little while later, he stops trying to defend himself. From that point on, it's just me whaling on this guy and teaching him the lesson he never learned in all those years he's been alive.

I'm like a man possessed because even when his face is so bloody I can't tell if I'm hitting a human or some kind of pathetic animal, I still keep beating him. It's like I can't stop.

But the truth is, I don't want to stop. This is how I've always wished I could feel but never found a way to achieve it. I've tried drugs and alcohol. I've tried all that happy talk bullshit my mother thinks helps. It never did.

This is what I've needed to feel good. If only I'd known this before tonight, I would have beat the hell out of someone already. This guy isn't the first person to make me want to lash out. He's just the unlucky son of a bitch who set me off on a night when something inside me said I wasn't going to stop myself anymore.

The sound of someone screaming pulls me out of my ecstasy, and I sit back on his bony legs as I drop my hands to my sides. The man lays beneath me a bloody mess, his body still and his eyes closed. I look around to see where the scream came from and see Kelsey running away.

Fucking girls. They always have to make a big deal out of everything.

I push my fingertips against the guy's shoulder to rouse him, but he doesn't move. That only pisses me off more, so I lean down and bark in his face, "Stop playing dead, asshole!"

He doesn't react at all, so I grab him by both shoulders and shake him. His head lolls back like some kind of oversized dandelion after the stem snaps, but he doesn't respond.

"Wake up! Stop being such a fucking pussy! I only hit you a few times. Wake the fuck up!" I yell in his face, but it does no good.

I press my fingertips to the side of his neck to feel for a pulse. A second goes by but I feel nothing. Then two. After ten seconds, I pull my hand away as I shake my head uncontrollably in disbelief.

He can't be dead. I only hit him a few times. What the fuck? Who dies from being hit in the face?

Panic races through me as I swivel my head left and right to see if anyone saw me. No one is there. Thank God. All I have to do is get up and run away as fast as I can, and nobody will know what happened.

I push myself off him and look around again to make

sure I'm alone. My heart's racing so fast I feel like I might puke. If anyone saw me, I'll go to jail.

Backing away from the body, I stumble over a rotting log and nearly fall, but I catch myself by grabbing onto a limb of a tree. I can't stop looking at him lying there.

Dead. Because of me.

I didn't mean to kill him. I only wanted to show him that he should leave people alone, for fuck's sake. We were only trying to have a good time out here in the woods. We weren't hurting anyone.

Then I remember Kelsey screaming. She saw me. She's probably running back to find her friend to tell her what happened.

I can't let her do that. Nobody can find out what I did.

She needs to know she has to keep her mouth shut.

THE PRESENT

I shake my head as water rolls down over my face. I'd hoped a shower would make me feel better, but my mind insisted on going back to that night nearly twenty years ago. I haven't thought about what I did for so long I think I convinced myself it never happened. That man ceased to exist that night because of my hands, and somehow my mind made him disappear over the years.

Until Bryan was murdered.

Nobody knows I killed that man. If anyone did, the police would have come to get me by now. It's been nearly two decades. If they knew, I would have been arrested before this since I know there's no statute of limitations for murder.

Then again, I made sure nobody knew. At least I thought I did.

I covered him up well enough, and then the six inches of snow that fell in the early season storm that came through the area a few days later made sure nobody would find him for at least a week. By that time, I'd made sure to tie up all the loose ends.

For all those years, I thought I'd gotten away with it. There was nobody to tell the police what happened because everyone who knew was gone.

Except for me.

Then tonight, I saw the face of someone who did know. All those years hadn't changed them enough to make me not recognize them the moment I saw them standing in front of me.

But that's impossible. There's no way she could have been at that gas station tonight. Or any other place, for that matter. She couldn't have been at the self-checkout at the supermarket or on the nature trail the other night.

I killed her to make sure she kept quiet. I know she was dead. I wouldn't have made a mistake like not checking before I buried her.

Yet it's like she's been haunting me. I don't know how, but it's her.

She's alive? How is that even possible?

Scrubbing my face as I let the shower rain over my head, I tell myself I'm losing my mind. Dead people do not show up nearly two decades later to haunt you at the grocery store and the gas station. That must have been someone else who looked like her. They say each of us has a twin somewhere in the world. That's it. It has to be.

Kelsey is still just as dead as I left her in the woods

that night, in a shallow grave that would have been covered over when it snowed just like the old man was. Whoever that woman was I've been seeing around town is just someone who looks like her. It has to be that.

It has to be because the only other choice means that terrible secret I've kept for all these years is going to come out.

CHAPTER TWENTY

amie

Closing my eyes, I let the sun warm my face after a long day at work. Contrary to what my husband thought, I was capable enough to find a job to support my girls and me. It's not easy work. My degree in human resources wasn't terribly valuable after not using anything I learned in college over all those years, so I had to start from scratch and find an entry-level job.

Our home isn't like the one we used to have too. That's okay. We may not have a pool anymore, but we can always go to my parents' house if we want to go swimming. We don't live in a community with an HOA either anymore. I don't miss that at all.

I came to realize the community I thought I had didn't exist. Not really. Oh, when we were living like everyone else with the perfectly manicured lawn courtesy of the landscaper and the home we could barely afford, our neighbors loved us. They joined us for parties and barbeques outside near the pool, smiling and laughing as they drank our alcohol and ate the delicious food I carefully prepared. As soon as trouble came our way, though, we weren't even good enough to say hello to anymore. That's not the kind of community I want for my girls and me.

We don't have as much of anything anymore, but what we do have we treasure. I make enough for the girls to still be in gymnastics, and now that what happened with Connor isn't news anymore and people have moved on, their teammates have returned to how they used to be with Cassandra and Danielle. For my daughters' parts, they've accepted their friendship, although I don't know if they see it as temporary like I do.

Even the mothers have accepted me again. Once they found out that Connor wasn't a great husband, they came around to understanding that whatever he did had nothing to do with me or our children. I'm polite when I see them, but now I know they were never truly my friends. They may want me to let them back in, but I've learned my lesson.

If it wasn't for Kelsey, I don't know if I would have made it through this past year. When everyone else abandoned me, she was there listening to me talk about my problems and offering help. She even loaned me the money to get the apartment the girls and I live in now.

"Mom, can we go swimming?"

I open my eyes and see my older daughter smiling

down at me. The late day sun behind her head makes her warm brown hair look like it has a golden halo behind it, like she's an angel.

"What does your grandmother say? I thought I heard her talking about having a cookout for dinner tonight."

My angel gives me a sly look and answers, "She hasn't started cooking anything yet, so Danielle and I thought we could hang out in the pool for a little while. I promise we won't give Grandma a hard time when she says it's time to come out."

She raises her hand in front of her like she's swearing in court. I shake my head, amused by how funny she can be.

"Okay, but remember, no giving Grandma any hassle."

Cassandra leans down and kisses my cheek. "Thanks, Mom!" As she runs away back into the house, I hear her yell, "She said we could! First one to the diving board wins!"

My daughters have handled this past year much better than I have. I don't know how, but it made them stronger. Danielle even stood up to some boy who kept teasing her about Connor. She never told me, but one night Cassandra mentioned it, and I was never prouder of the two of them than I was that night.

As for my marriage, that was a casualty of Connor's mistake. Once the police determined it had to be him who killed Bryan, there was little left between the two of us. He wanted me to ignore the truth and stay loyal to him. I couldn't. The truth made it impossible.

Next week, he goes on trial for the murder of Bryan Corsei. I know because those terrible reporters have started contacting me again. I thought I'd made it through that horrible experience and put it behind me, but they've returned again in the past couple weeks.

The sharks smell blood in the water, and they're circling.

I've got nothing to say to them. I still can't believe this is what our life turned into, but I can't deny the truth any longer. Connor killed that poor man. I don't know why. Maybe it was jealousy like the prosecutors say. I did hear him complain that Bryan was the favorite of their boss more than once.

It took me a long time to come around to believing the man I married could do such a dreadful thing. Kelsey says that even people we would never suspect of anything heinous can have a secret side to them. She must be right.

Cuppa Cuppa is especially busy this morning, but it is a Saturday, so that's probably why. Now that I work Monday through Friday, I've come to genuinely appreciate weekends. Before all of this happened, they were simply the days of the week I cleaned the house or had the girls' friends over. Now, I see those two days off in a different light.

Kelsey waves from the back of the coffee shop, so I give the girl behind the counter a quick smile before going back to join my friend. Our schedules are filled to the brim, but we take time out every Saturday to catch up and chat for a few hours.

"You look great today, Jamie! Doing something new

with your hair?" she asks as I hang my purse off the back of the chair and sit down.

I smooth whatever fly-aways there are on the top of my head and smile. "Nothing new. To be honest, I think I need to get a haircut, but I just can't find the time. I'm getting my usual. Do you need anything?"

She shakes her head. "No, I'm good. Thanks!"

After grabbing my iced latte and a blueberry scone heated and buttered, I head back to the table where Kelsey is sitting grinning at me. She looks like the cat that just ate the canary, so of course, I'm curious what she's so happy about today.

"What's this about?" I ask as I playfully point at her face.

She shrugs and shakes her head. "Nothing. I'm just so happy with how everything turned out. You've done so well for yourself, Jamie, and after the year you've had, I think you deserve congratulations. Other people would have crumbled under the weight of everything you had to deal with, but you didn't, and I'm proud of you."

Beaming a smile after her kind words, I feel as happy as she looks. "Thank you! It was hard. I felt guilty about not standing by Connor, but I had to keep my girls' happiness uppermost in my mind. To be honest, you get the credit for that. I didn't have the guts to stand up for them, but that day you told me I had to do what was right for them made me realize I needed to be their champion. I'm sorry for what's likely to happen to Connor. I really am. I just had to do what any good mother would and protect my daughters."

Kelsey raises her plastic iced latte cup and taps it off of mine. "To Jamie and her strength!"

I'll take it. There's been so much bad these past twelve months that any good that comes my way I welcome with open arms.

"If I'm being honest, you deserve a toast as much as I do. I don't know what I would have done if you weren't around, Kelsey. When everyone decided I deserved to be treated as a leper, you were there for me. I don't think I can ever repay you for that."

She waves away any suggestion I owe her anything for her friendship. "Nonsense. I did what any decent person would do. Whatever your husband did or didn't do, that's up to a jury to decide. You aren't Connor. You're your own person who deserves to be treated with respect. I can't say what's wrong with all those people you've told me about who abandoned you as soon as the rumors started about him killing that man, but I'll say this. They didn't deserve your friendship."

I raise my cup and mimic what she did a minute ago. "To friendship! And thank you so much for being my friend."

People begin to sit at the open tables around us making the coffee shop quite noisy, so we fall into a comfortable silence only good friends understand. I can't help but think back on the past year and my friendship with Kelsey. I can't count the times I felt so down, so deserted by everyone in my world that I barely dragged myself out of bed. I didn't have a choice, though. I had to for my girls.

And all along, Kelsey was there to support me every step of the way. She listened to everything I had to say about Connor, the good and the bad, and she never judged me. Unlike all those phony friends, she understood I didn't deserve blame for what my husband did.

"Hey, you look a million miles away over there. Everything okay?" she sweetly asks.

I nod, happy that answer isn't a lie anymore. "Yeah. I'm good. I was just thinking about everything that happened this past year. Who knew so much could be stuffed into three hundred and sixty-five days?"

Giving my hand a gentle squeeze, she sighs. "I'm hoping for your sake and your daughters' sake that this coming year is going to be better. You aren't going to the trial, are you?"

That answer doesn't take any thought at all. I shake my head quickly because that's the last place on earth I want to go.

"No. Connor refuses to speak to me since I filed for divorce, so I don't see any reason why I'd go. If I thought it would bring him some peace, I'd be right there for him because even though I know he did it, I still think he deserves a friendly face nearby. He's so full of hate for me right now, though, that it would probably only upset him."

She nods in that way that shows she cares and gives my hand another soft squeeze. "My mother always said you have to let people feel what they need to feel. He's angry now, but I hope in the future he'll see you did what you had to so those beautiful daughters of yours could be happy."

"All he ever says is I left him when he needed me

most. I don't know how this makes me look, but I've never regretted leaving. I had to protect my girls."

"And yourself. You always put yourself last, Jamie. I say for this coming year your goal should be putting yourself first for once."

When she says things like that, and she has a few times recently, I always instantly feel guilty. I've tried to put Cassandra and Danielle first from the day they were born. I don't know how to change that.

"I'm not sure I know how," I say, not ashamed that I love my girls but feeling foolish that as a woman in the twenty-first century I don't know how to put myself first.

Kelsey nods. "I get it. I had a hard time doing that too. For years, I felt like I was being selfish putting myself first, but ask yourself this. How good will you be for your children if you aren't your best?"

I think about that for a few seconds and answer, "Not much, I guess."

"You can't do for others who need you when your cup is empty, Jamie. It's not selfish to take care of yourself. Even more, your daughters will learn an important lesson if you do. They'll see they need to put themselves first too. You'll be teaching them how to treat themselves better. I wish someone had taught us that."

She's always so smart when we talk about things like this. I've gotten so used to her that I rarely even notice her scars anymore, but I have a feeling what caused them has made her see she had to look out for herself.

I remember her mentioning her husband a while back, but she rarely talks about him. Once she mentioned she met him after the terrible thing that happened to her all those years ago. He must be an incredible person to look past her scars to see the great person beneath them.

"So let's switch gears. Have you considered dating any time soon? I know your divorce isn't final yet, but it's something to think about. You're still young."

A nervous chuckle explodes out of me when I think about getting back into the dating world again. "Oh, God. I haven't really given it any thought. There's a guy at the store I work at who's always nice. I thought maybe he might ask me out sometime, but so far, it's just been friendly comments on break when we see one another."

I stop and then add, "Anyway, I think I should probably wait until the divorce is final. It won't be much longer now. Connor is too worried about his upcoming trial to drag his feet anymore. We don't have to haggle over custody or visitation, so at least there's that. But I'm not sure I'm ready to get back into dating just yet. I've got a lot of baggage. I'm not sure any man would want to deal with that."

Kelsey's mouth turns down into a deep frown. "What Connor did isn't your fault. You share no blame for that. Any man who thinks you do isn't the right one for you."

Quickly, I work to make sure she knows I wasn't meaning that. "Oh, no. I was talking about having two daughters. Many men don't want a ready-made family right out of the gate. It's okay. I don't mind being alone for now. It's a new start for me, and I'm enjoying the freedom of it being just me and my girls."

"Well, I can get behind that too. Men can wait. Right now, it's all about the Year of Jamie. I like that!"

The Year of Jamie. I think I love the sound of that, especially after the year I've just had.

CHAPTER TWENTY-ONE

elsey

THREE MONTHS LATER

MY HUSBAND SQUEEZES MY HAND TIGHTLY AS WE drive down the highway on a beautiful summer day. I look over at him and smile, knowing he wants this to happen as much as I do.

It's been a long time waiting for this day. Years of tears and heartache during which I was sure this would never happen.

But it had to. Nothing stays buried forever. Even Connor should have realized that.

I doubt he thought much about what he did over all these years. He was living the life he thought he deserved, happy to move away from that small town right outside of Pittsburgh where his actions that terrible October night set our future in stone.

When I first saw his face after all this time, I thought I might be sick. He looked so content. He had a nice job, a great house, a beautiful wife, and two lovely daughters. He lived in a gated community, so he never had to deal with the people he believed are beneath him.

Time has been kind to him too, strangely enough. I had hoped it would have ravaged the outside of him like I had wished guilt would do to his insides, but one glance at that smooth, tanned face showed me time had given him a gift it didn't give me.

One he doesn't deserve.

"We're almost there. You okay?" my husband asks as he gives my hand another gentle squeeze.

He's been so good all these years with all I've had to go through. The months in the hospital after they found me half-buried in the woods. So many surgeries to repair my face, most of which haven't done what I prayed for but only did little to fix the damage from being beaten nearly to death.

You see, there were two victims that night. That old man Connor insisted on going after and me. I made the mistake of looking for him to make sure he was okay, and he returned my kindness by savagely attacking me. I didn't understand then, but I've come to over the years.

I was a witness to his heinous crime, so he had to get rid of me. He thought he did too. With his fists, he pummeled my face over and over until I must have been unrecognizable. Then he wrapped his hands around my neck and squeezed the life out of me until I blacked out.

He thought I was dead. He thought he'd gotten rid of the only person who knew what he'd done. So he buried me in a shallow grave, but by the grace of God himself, someone came along and interrupted him, making it necessary for him to abandon me only half-hidden under the rotting leaves and dirt he intended to make my final resting place.

I swear I can still smell the earthy scent of death that filled my nostrils for hours that night. It haunts me to this day. I always wear perfume to keep it from invading my senses, but sometimes no matter how much I put on, that terrible smell still overwhelms me.

Closing my eyes, I lift my wrist to my nose and inhale deeply. Today, I wore the perfume my husband loves. He says it makes him think of that week we spent at the beach right after we started dating. He has lots of happy memories of our time together.

I wish I did, but I've spent most of the past two decades wishing I looked different, not the scarred mess I see every time I see myself in a mirror. Before that fateful night, I used to admire myself in anything that would show me a reflection. Mirrors. Windows. Anything that showed me how beautiful I was.

That changed that night. Since then, I avoid looking at myself as much as I can. Mornings are the hardest because that's when I have to stare into the mirror as I do my hair. Even those fifteen minutes a day make me sick to my stomach. If I could do it with my eyes closed, I would. Anything to avoid seeing what I look like.

I wish I could see myself through my husband's eyes. He somehow sees a beautiful woman he loves. Or at least that's what he tells me. I don't think he lies so much as sees what he wants instead of what's really there.

My mind drifts back to that terrible night when my life changed forever. If I'm being honest, the person I was disappeared that night.

With each step I take, I want to scream. Where is Samantha? We need to get back to her car and head to her grandmother's house. I don't care if she's hitting it off with that guy she went off with. Mine's a psycho, and the sooner I get away from him, the better.

Thank God for the full moon tonight, or I don't think I'd be able to see two feet in front of me in these woods. "Samantha!" I say in the loudest whisper I can manage. "Come on. We need to go. Where are you?"

I get no response. Where can she be?

The sound of a branch snapping behind me makes me spin around in panic, and I see a squirrel race past me as my heart nearly explodes out of my chest. Damn flying rat! Go to sleep and stop scaring me.

"Samantha! Please answer me! We need to get out of here right now," I say, wishing I could do more than loudly whisper, but I don't want Connor to know where I am. The last thing I need now is to have to deal with him.

Footsteps come up behind me so fast that I barely have time to turn around, and a second later, he's on me. He takes me to the ground, and for a split second, it feels playful, like we're being silly out here.

But then I look up into his eyes and see it's not playing he has on his mind.

"Connor! Let me go!" I cry out loudly, hoping his friends and Samantha will hear me.

The first time his fist slams into my face he splits my lower lip wide open. I've never been hit in the face before, and it stuns me for a moment or two. I don't get a chance to recover before his fist crashes into my cheekbone next. Pain radiates up through my eye, and all I want to do is cry.

"Stop! Don't do this!" I sob and flail my hands to stop him, but it's like he's a man possessed and nothing I'm saying is making it through the haze of his rage.

Over and over, he punches me until I can barely feel it. I continue to scream for him to stop and let me go, but he never responds, never even acknowledges what I'm saying to him.

It's like I'm not even here, except for the fact that he keeps attacking me.

Then he stops for a second or two, and I see him lean over toward my right side. Is he done? I try to listen for sounds of anyone coming to help me, but all I hear are birds in the distance making screeching noises.

Suddenly, he rises up, and I watch in horror as he lifts his arm to continue beating me, but now he holds a rock in his hand! I turn my head to avoid it, and he slams it into my cheekbone, ripping the skin wide open. I feel myself fading away with each time the rock smashes my face.

Finally, he sits back on my legs and looks down at me. The hate in his eyes terrifies me, but I need to try to reach him before he begins hitting me again.

"Connor, please let me go. I promise I won't say a word to anyone. I swear. Just let me go. Please."

Blood seeps out of my mouth and down my chin as I speak. Everything hurts as I stare up at him and hope I can reach some part of Connor that understands what I'm saying.

When he finally says something, my heart drops. "I won't let you ruin my life. That guy shouldn't be dead. I just hit him a few *times. But I won't go to jail for a mistake. I won't let you do that to me."*

I open my mouth to say I won't tell a soul what I saw, but before I can get a word out, he lunges toward me, wrapping his hands around my throat. Pure terror rushes through me as I feel his fingers press into my flesh just below my ears and I begin to gag.

Shaking my head frantically, I try to make it impossible for him to choke me, but he tightens his hold, almost as if he's punishing me for trying to stay alive. I claw at his hands to get free, but he's too strong and to desperate to silence me.

Slowly, I feel myself slipping away. My eyelids close as the end inches closer. All I wanted to do was have some fun tonight, and I'm going to die because of that. This bastard is going to take my life right here in these woods on this chilly October night. He's going to kill me, and everything I've ever dreamed of will be taken from me.

Going to college to be a TV news reporter.

Getting married someday and having children.

Seeing my parents again and one day watching them love being grandparents.

He's going to take all of that from me.

Then, just as I'm sure I only have seconds left in this world, Connor's hands leave my throat. I'm too scared to open my eyes to see his expression or what he intends to do next, so I stay still and play dead, praying to God he won't check my pulse.

A moment later, he lifts himself up off my legs, and as much as I know this may be my last chance to get away, I can't move. All I want to do is sleep.

Just sleep.

When I finally open my eyes, I'm alone. Leaves and dirt cover me, filling my nose with the earthy scent of decay. I used to love this smell. When I was a little girl, I loved when my father would rake the fall leaves into a pile and let me jump into them. I'd giggle and throw the leaves high in the air as my father took pictures.

I'll never smell this scent again without hating it. It's nothing but putrid to me now.

Too afraid to move in case he's still nearby, I take shallow breaths that hurt my throat, thankful to be alive. Everything on my body hurts, especially my head. My face feels swollen, but I can't tell for sure. A sharp pain in my lower abdomen sends waves of utter agony coursing through me. I've never experienced anything like this.

All I know is I'm alive. That's all that matters.

Those birds from a few minutes ago seem closer now. The noises they make remind me of shrieks of horror. It's the perfect soundtrack for what I've endured.

I hear voices in the distance calling out like they're underwater. They say my name, but I can't respond. I have no voice now.

Leaves and twigs cover my arms and legs, and dirt lays on top of me. He buried me, thinking I was dead. He buried me so I'd never be found again.

He thought he killed me, but I survived.

"You're quiet. That's never a good thing, Kelsey. Talk to me."

My husband always knows when I'm getting lost in my own head, a dangerous place to be for someone like me. In his sweet way, he somehow always manages to rescue me before I get in too deep. If he didn't, I'd drown in those terrible thoughts I can't seem to stop.

I look over at him and smile. He isn't looking at me, so I feel okay doing that.

"Just thinking. I never thought this day would come. You did, though, didn't you?"

He glances over at me and nods. "I was going to do anything I could to make sure it did. You know that, right?"

I don't answer, but I give his hand a squeeze to let him know I never doubted him for a second. The justice system? I doubted it would ever catch up to Connor. But not my husband. Not the person who's been with me every day since the horrible events of that night and all the terrible things that followed.

I wish Samantha could be here with us. She should be since she suffered as much as I did because of that night. Never able to overcome the guilt she felt for letting me go with someone like Connor, she lived in torture before taking her own life right after Christmas three years later. I never wanted that for her, but no matter what I said, she could never shake the feeling that she was to blame for what happened to me.

She was wrong, though. She didn't ruin my life.

He did.

And now he's going to pay.

After parking the car, we walk along the sidewalk surrounding the courthouse. My husband holds my hand and brings it up to his mouth to place a kiss on my knuckles. He's sweet like that. Always has been. I saw that in him the first time I met him that terrible night.

"Are you ready for this?" he asks as he stops the two of us before we walk up the stairs into the building.

I nod, suddenly feeling like I'm going to burst into tears. I hadn't expected this to be so emotional. For months, we made our plan to get revenge on Connor.

Then nothing went right. First, I was careless and let him see me at the grocery store. I worried that may have ruined everything we had planned.

Then we followed him that day when he went hiking, but before my husband could carry out his plan to attack him, the man he was with started waving that gun around. Of course, once he shot himself, Connor ran away like the coward he is, leaving his friend to bleed to death.

Yes, his friend accidentally committed suicide. So why didn't the coroner see that? Why did he rule it a homicide?

Fate helped with that in the name of my cousin, Joseph Murray. It was he who alerted me to the fact that Connor had moved to that community. One day, the phone rang, and there he was giving me the news that would change my life.

And Connor's.

My cousin knew what I had endured. The multiple surgeries to repair my face that never quite did the job. The years of therapy to help me come to grips with the horrors I experienced that night. The loss of my friend and the guilt that came from her taking her life.

He knew and sympathized with me. Then one day, my revenge landed on his examination table. Bryan Corsei and the unfortunate circumstances of his death would finally give me the closure I'd always wanted.

A just ending for someone who deserved so much worse.

Even more than my cousin helping, all of the people in Connor's life helped bring about his fate. Just as I had endured people's hurtful whispers and judgments since that terrible night, as soon as there was even a hint that he wasn't the great guy he pretended to be, they went after him. I have to admit they surprised me with how fast they turned on him. Unfortunately, they turned on his wife and daughters, but all Jamie had to do was put a little distance between them and Connor and everyone saw they didn't deserve any of the attacks.

I never wanted to hurt her or the girls. In fact, I can't tell you how many times I had to force myself not to tell Jamie what kind of man her husband really was for all those years. That wouldn't have worked, though. I've seen countless women defend rotten men from rumors of bad behavior in my lifetime. No, it was necessary that she see who Connor really was all on her own. Only then would she understand she needed to abandon him to save herself and her girls.

Today, my husband and I will watch as the jury comes back with their sentence. Connor was found guilty of murder, mostly because he was too cheap and too cocky to hire a good lawyer. If he had, he may have gotten off since a decent attorney would have been able to at least cast doubt on my cousin's coroner report.

Now we find out how long Connor will spend in prison. Not that it will ever be long enough to make up for the murder of that poor old man and what he did to me and what his actions made Samantha do to herself. If he spends every day of his life behind bars from today on, that still won't bring two people back to life and give me all I could have had.

But I've learned that you have to deal with what you're handed in this world. Sometimes it's the worst thing you can imagine, but through it all, there can be some happiness. You just have to let it in.

Rich cradles my scarred face in his hands and smiles down at me. "I'm right here with you just like I have been since that night. We've waited for him to get what he deserves, and today the wait is finally over. No matter what that jury comes back with, he'll finally pay for what he did."

I nod, loving the feel of his palms resting against my cheeks. "I know. I've been thinking we're lucky. I never wanted you to be tainted by all of this, and when yet another person died around Connor, it all came together. I'm just thankful Joseph did what he did so you didn't have to do anything."

He smiles and leans down to softly kiss my lips. "I didn't care what I had to do to make him pay, Kelsey. I'm glad your cousin could help, but I was ready to do what had to be done so Connor Jennings pays. He had to suffer for all he did. He had to."

I nod and walk up the courthouse stairs as I remember Connor has had nearly twenty years of the life he wanted. He got the nice house, the beautiful wife, and the lovely children. He got the admiration of his community and his coworkers.

He got all the things I had dreamed of and that he stole from me that terrible night for nearly twenty undeserved years.

Sometimes I wonder what all our lives would have been like if Samantha and I hadn't stopped at that convenience store on her way to her grandmother's house. Would she still be alive because she didn't blame herself for what happened to me? Would I be the television news reporter I dreamed of becoming in high school?

For all the horrible things that sprang from that night, one wonderful surprise did come out of it. Rich has been the rock in my life I needed. He didn't have to step up and give me support when I was in the hospital and unsure I'd ever see the day Connor would pay for all he did. Or maybe he did because of the man he is.

I didn't tell him the truth of what happened to me for nearly five years, but I think he suspected his friend was guilty all along because he never told him what happened to me that night. He let him believe I'd left him alone in those woods. My husband wanted to tell the police that day I finally felt comfortable enough to share my story, but I didn't.

Telling the police would mean I would have to go through a trial, and I knew I'd be dragged through the mud by Connor's defense in their attempt to save him. I couldn't risk that. Connor Jennings looked like a golden boy with the job and the house and the family to show he couldn't possibly be the person to leave me for dead after beating me senseless.

No, I wasn't going to let any slick attorneys put me on trial. There had to be a better way of getting him to pay for what he did to me and that poor old man that night.

And then one night as I lay in bed wondering what my life would have been like if only I hadn't met him that night, it came to me. He had to lose everything, and I had to make sure of that. In the middle of one of the worst times of my life, I finally figured it out.

I had to be the one who exacted revenge.

Rich and I take our seats in the back of the courtroom where Connor's fate will be decided. I see him at the defense table and notice he isn't smiling like he was during the trial. Well, all the time except at that perfect moment when the jury found him guilty of killing Bryan Corsei. Then he looked like the pathetic man I always knew he was.

The female judge enters the room and sits down before the jury of five men and seven women files in and takes their seats in the jury box. As my heart pounds in my chest, I listen as the foreperson announces Connor's fate. I tighten my hold on Rich's hand and hold my breath as she goes through the necessary information about the case and then says the most satisfying words I've ever heard. Not the most beautiful or any I love the most. Those belong to my wonderful husband.

No, hearing that woman with the short gray hair and soft voice say Connor Jennings will spend the rest of his life in prison fills me with utter satisfaction. He finally will get to experience what I've lived through for all these years. If there's any justice in the world, he'll get to spend twice as long as that behind bars.

Rich looks over at me and smiles. "Ready to go?"

I nod and stand to leave just as I watch Connor turn around. When he sees me, his eyes open wide in utter shock. You thought you killed me that night, you son of a bitch, but I hung on until someone found me. Now you get to know what it feels like to be trapped in a life you never wanted.

The last thing I see is the sheriff slap the handcuffs on him and lead him away to prison. He looks back one final time, and I give him a smile just like I did that night when he came running toward me after beating that old man to death.

That's for him, for me, for Samantha, and for everyone you hurt in this life, Connor.

I notice his wife and daughters aren't in the courtroom as we turn to walk out. In fact, there's no one seated on his side of the courtroom.

A fitting end for a killer.

ABOUT THE AUTHOR

K.M. Scott loves a good story. A New York Times and USA Today bestselling author, K.M. has written dozens of books. In addition to romance, she's written cozy mysteries under her Anina Collins pen name. She lives in Pennsylvania with a herd of animals and when she's not writing can be found reading or feeding her TV addiction.

Be sure to visit K.M.'s Facebook page at **https://www.facebook.com/kmscottauthor** for all the latest on her books, along with giveaways and other goodies! And to hear all the news on K.M. Scott books first, sign up for her newsletter today and be sure to visit her website at **http://www.kmscottbooks.com**

Temptation (Club X #1)

Surrender (Club X #2)

Possession (Club X #3)

Satisfaction (Club X #4)

Acceptance (Club X #5)

Complete Club X Series Box Set

NeXt SERIES

Notorious (NeXt #1)

Infamous (NeXt #2)

Ravenous (NeXt #3)

Ambitious (NeXt #4)

Flirtatious (NeXt #5)

Mysterious (NeXt #6)

Sensuous (NeXt #7)

Desirous (NeXt #8)

KING BROTHERS SERIES

Cruel King

Wild King

Broken King

Lone King

CORRUPTED LOVE TRILOGY

If I Dream (Corrupted Love #1)

If You Fight (Corrupted Love #2)

If We Fall (Corrupted Love #3)

Corrupted Love Trilogy Box Set

ADDICTED TO YOU SERIES

Crave (Addicted To You #1)

Adore (Addicted To You #2)

Shatter (Addicted To You #3)

Claim (Addicted To You #4)

Addicted To You Series Box Set

PROJECT ARTEMIS SERIES

In The Darkness (Project Artemis #1)

After The Storm (Project Artemis #2)

Behind The Scenes (Project Artemis #3)

Project Artemis Box Set

FINDING THE ONE SERIES

Hard Work (Finding The One #1)

Big Love (Finding The One #2)

DIRTY BOSS SERIES

Sweet Things (Dirty Boss #1)

Private Secretary (Dirty Boss #2)

Play Date (Dirty Boss #3)

Dirty Boss Volume One

ALSO BY K.M. SCOTT WRITING AS ANINA COLLINS

POPPY MCGUIRE COZY MYSTERY SERIES

The Eleventh Hour

After Hours

Top of the Hour

The Darkest Hour

Happy Hour

The Witching Hour

The Finest Hour

Poppy McGuire Mysteries Box Set #1

Poppy McGuire Mysteries Box Set #2